The Sighting

Christopher Coleman

Description

The Sighting

EVERY FOURTEEN MONTHS it appears on a secluded beach in a small town just before dawn.

One morning during his daily run to the beach, Danny Lynch witnesses the strangest and most incredible thing he's ever seen.

A dark, man-like figure emerges from the ocean, stands for just a few moments on the beach, and then retreats back to the surf. Danny's perspective on the world changes in an instant, and as the only eyewitness to this event, his mission now is to convince anyone who will listen that what he saw was real. But with only a vague photo and a dubious story, that task is proving almost impossible, and his only hope may be in finding a mysterious woman who was at the beach earlier that morning, and who may hold the terrifying secret that could cost Danny his life.

Chapter 1

DANNY LYNCH KEPT HIS shoulders high and wide and then turned sharply off the asphalt jogging path, striding east now on the planks of the beach access. As his soles hit the wooden planks, he was instantly grateful for the softer feel of the boardwalk on the bottoms of his feet, and he closed his eyes for a moment, savoring the sensation as he increased his speed. He opened his eyes again and was now close enough that he could just make out the bottom landing of the stairway that led up to the ocean overlook. He turned his gallop into a sprint, determined to end this run—as every run—with the last drops of fuel left in his tank.

Danny reached the sandy landing like a wild dog, panting and dishevelled, and then began his ascent of the stairway, staring down towards his feet, shortening his steps as he pumped his knees high, deliberate with each march, careful both to maximize every muscle in his legs and to keep from slipping on the treacherous incline. He turned his focus forward now, craning his neck toward the welcoming arms of the railings above him and the dark sky that was just beginning to blossom to blue.

He reached the top of the overlook with a fury, stomping out the last two steps on the boards that formed the floor, and then unleashed a low-pitch grunt that was some hybrid of scream and growl. He put his hands on top of his head and eased into the first stages of his wind-down routine, pacing the square, boxing-ring-sized overlook, moving his hands to his hips now and thrusting his chest forward, full and proud, taking in full breaths of the cool morning air before puffing them out toward the beach. As always, he was thankful to be done with this part of his daily regimen. He looked at his watch—6:47 am.

Danny unshouldered his backpack onto one of the overlook benches that bordered the square, unlatched the fold-over cover, and pulled out his bathing suit, laying it out in front of him next to the backpack. He quickly undressed, stripping entirely naked for just a moment before stepping his legs into the

2

swimsuit. He tied the suit tight and left his clothes on the bench next to a nylon bag, which he brought everyday for his wet things, and then began his slow descent toward the beach.

He touched down on the sand just as a bright orange wedge formed on the horizon. He headed towards it, appreciating the cool dry grains that flowed between his toes as he ran.

Danny reached the water's edge and continued into the surf without breaking stride, never giving the cold ocean a chance to make him rethink his morning dip. The salt water rushed quickly over his groin and waist, then his torso and shoulders, before Danny ducked his head forward into one of the relentless waves that had been peppering this beach for untold millions of years. He held his breath and stayed under the water for what seemed like two minutes, but was probably closer to thirty seconds, before exploding up, breaching the surface like some tiny humpback whale.

This had been Danny Lynch's practice for five months now, six days a week, with only a few exceptional days when the weather had simply not cooperated. Otherwise, he ran the 3.7 miles to the beach, swam for ten or fifteen minutes (except on the winteriest of winter mornings when he'd barely allow time for the water to get him wet), allowed himself time to dry on the sand as he watched the sun rise, and then ran the 3.7 miles home. Living within five miles of the beach and a dip in the ocean every day: those were two things on the list of a dozen that made up Danny's dream life, a list he'd first started compiling about four years earlier.

And now here he was doing it, living those bullets on his list—this one at least—honing his body and spirit in the process, and not for anyone or thing in particular, but rather to increase his own feeling of self-worth. He was as fit as he'd ever been in his life. And it felt great.

The rest of his life, however, was still a work in progress. In certain ways, the money had given him freedom; in others, it held him back.

Perhaps it had come too easy. He'd written one song, that was all, and only the lyrics mind you, not the music, which Danny always admitted was the much more difficult part of the equation. Most people he knew could rhyme a few words and create two or three double entendres, but there were far fewer who could form the melody behind those words.

But the deal was deal, right from the beginning: if any money ever came from "Full-blown Superstar," the split would be 50/50. And when the song reached number three on the Billboard Top 40, that money became fairly significant. It was amazing what one hit could pay off over time, especially when it was used in a couple of commercials and one bad movie. And he still heard it quite often on television, playing in the background of an arena or stadium, being used as a device to pump up the crowds at various sporting events.

And the royalty checks just never seemed to stop flowing in. He wasn't a millionaire, per se, it hadn't quite reached that level, but last year he'd cleared six-hundred thousand dollars and hadn't really done a day's work.

Danny stood in the water with his knees bent, keeping his shoulders beneath the surface while he stared at the horizon and the sun's emergence beyond it. This was a gift to live this life, he thought, but then immediately shooed the notion from his mind, returning instead to the reality of the sunrise. Stay in the present and just focus on what's happening now. He must have recited that refrain to himself twenty times a day. It was a tough path to stay on, but it was good self-advice. Life always seemed a bit better when he followed it.

He dipped his head once more beneath the water line and then propelled his body forward toward the beach, pushing off with his toes from the soft, oily sand and emerging tall into waist-high water, shaking off the chill as he rose.

And then he saw her.

She was blurry through the prism of water droplets, a figure just off to his left, standing on the dunes, slightly shrouded by the tall bent grass. Danny wiped the ocean from his eyes and watched her; she was staring with intensity, straight ahead but not at him. Her aim was the beach, or perhaps the water beyond, and he could see that the newly-risen sun was reflecting in her eyes a look of concern. Alarm even. He turned to look at the object of her gaze, and as he did, he thought he caught a glimpse of her head turning toward him. Danny searched in the direction of her stare for several moments but could see only sand and water, and when he turned back to the dunes, the woman was gone.

He walked up toward the beach grass, in the direction of where the mysterious woman had been standing only seconds ago, and looked down off the dunes that sloped back past the beachfront homes. But she was gone. Almost impossibly.

The land around him was flat and open, so if she had sprinted away—which would have been odd, but Danny accepted the possibility—he would have seen her retreating somewhere in the distance.

He supposed she could have lived in one of the homes that lined the dunes, and after seeing him, had quickly meandered back through the tall grass and into the safety of her house. But why?

Danny took a deep breath and shook his head quickly, bringing his focus back to the moment once again. He scoffed at his imagination, quietly embarrassed by both his interest in the woman and his excessive concern about where she'd gone. What was he so intrigued by anyway? A woman staring out at the ocean at seven in the morning wasn't at all unusual. And perhaps she hadn't noticed that he was there at first, and when she finally did see him, she became uncomfortable and left quickly. Maybe she'd even hid from him. Perhaps she'd been assaulted at one point in her life and wasn't taking any chances. These were all reasonable explanations for the moment he'd just experienced.

But it also didn't feel right.

He had caught a glimpse of something in her eyes, before she'd known he was there. Something that resembled fear. And she wasn't just staring at the horizon; she was looking at something specific. Or, perhaps, for something specific. He could see it in her posture. Hers was no snugly cup-of-coffee moment, one arm hugging her chest while deep in existential thought. No, there was a searching there. A telling pose. A rise in the shoulders. A lean forward and craning of the neck.

Danny turned back toward the water and let his gaze rest on the ebbing waves as he continued to look in the general direction of where the woman had been staring. He didn't notice anything unusual, and as the moment waned, he slowly began to ease the woman from his mind as he walked back toward the stairs that led to up to the landing.

He ruffled his hair dry with his hands and then brought his hands down across his face as he reached the landing. He took two steps up, and that's when he heard the sound explode behind him.

Sploosh!

The sound was as violent as a car crash, like an open refrigerator had been dropped from a helicopter and had landed front first into the ocean.

Danny spun toward the sound, staring back to the place where he'd been only seconds earlier. He saw his towel on the beach—he forgot it at least once a month—but at first glance, he detected nothing in the dark dawn waters.

And then he saw it began to emerge.

It materialized slowly at first, just thirty yards or so from the shore, a form so black it looked to be the shadow of some other figure, one flying above the water perhaps. But there was no sun above to create shadows, and as the black object rose higher above the surface of the water, gradually plodding forward toward the beach with every step, there was no doubt in Danny's mind that what he was seeing was something three-dimensional and real.

It reached the water's edge, where it slapped its feet down on the shoreline, stopping just at the point on the sand where the tide would continue nipping at its heels. It walked erect on two legs, this thing that had the general shape and limbs of a man. But what man could this be? It was enormous. Danny estimated whatever was standing there on the shores of Rove Beach, perhaps less than fifty yards from him, must have stood seven feet tall. At least. But even more impressive than its height was its build. It was almost gorilla-like in its mass, but unlike a gorilla, it stood tall, and its body appeared hairless. Danny was too far away and the hour still too dark to tell if there were scales or skin covering the thing, but whatever formed the outer layer of the creature made it look like a walking void of blackness.

Danny's first instinct was to scream, to call out to any passerby who might happen to be in the general vicinity, perhaps the first of today's beachgoers who would shuffle hurriedly towards his voice and bear witness to this discovery. But shouting was sure to cause one of two reactions from the giant black form: it would either retreat back to the ocean, leaving no evidence that it had ever stood there in the first place; or it would turn toward him, perhaps run with the pace of a bear and maul Danny before he ever reached the top of the overlook. He wasn't in any immediate danger, he decided, and the notion to shout suddenly seemed foolish and cowardly.

His next thought was to flee, make a run for it, one short deliberate burst up to the overlook and his awaiting phone. At that point, he could either call someone or take pictures with the camera, immortalizing proof of this extraordinary morning.

But for the moment, his muscles refuted both notions. So instead, Danny just stood on the bottom landing and watched the giant marine creature as it stood at the edge of the Atlantic, standing tall, staring up at the dunes.

It moved closer up the beach, just a few steps, and then stopped, going no further than the tide. It raised its head now, and Danny thought it was about to bellow, unleashing some angry Kong-like cry to the world, calling out for some unrequited love or lost child. But it stayed silent, instead moving its head back and forth, scanning the dunes, until, as it reached the farthest right point in its side-to-side swivel, exactly in the direction of Danny, it stopped.

It was smelling, Danny now considered, searching for a scent, and it had picked up his. Or perhaps it had heard him breathing, detecting him with some type of superhuman sonar. Whatever sense the thing was using, Danny was suddenly exposed, possibly threatened, even with the distance between them.

When the beast was blind to him, unaware, Danny felt almost like he was observing an animal at the zoo. But now that it had seemed to notice him, or at least detect his presence, Danny felt in the crosshairs.

He sized up the man-thing one last time, and based on its height and girth, and Danny's own running acumen and distance from the beast, he calculated that, even if the thing turned for him, he could outrun it. Perhaps not for more than a few hundred feet, but long enough that he could find cover. This calculation wasn't a mathematical given, but it was a reasonable estimation.

And also, he thought, *what the fuck is that thing*!

Danny took three or four slow steps backwards in the direction of the stairs, testing the thing's reaction to his movements. The creature tilted its head up once at the movement, but its feet stayed planted. Danny began moving more quickly now, steadily in reverse, his eyes never leaving the giant ocean animal. In less than ten seconds, Danny had made his way up to the midway landing where he stopped again, positioning himself behind a portion of the deck's railing, believing in some abstract way that the thin strip of rotting wood could somehow protect him if things suddenly deteriorated.

But it would never be put to the test.

Without cue or hesitation, the creature suddenly pivoted its head toward the dunes, stared for a few seconds longer, and then turned back around toward the water. Danny absently labeled the creature's motion one of disappointment, as if the thing had been promised some gift that never came to pass.

It took several huge strides toward the ocean, lingered for a moment at the edge of the surf, and then, facing due east now with its head high and level with the horizon, as quickly as it had emerged, began to step back into the ocean.

Danny took a breath and blinked for the first time in what felt like minutes. He was out of harm's way and would live to see another day. Both of those things were no sure thing less than five minutes ago. He took two more deep, deliberate breaths, trying to keep from hyperventilating as he watched the thing ease slowly back to the ocean.

And then panic set it.

"Shit," he whispered. "Shit, no!"

Danny pushed himself off the railing, and with the same urgency he would have had if the creature were actually chasing him, he scaled the remaining steps up to the landing, two at a time, reaching the top and grabbing his backpack almost in a single motion.

"No, no, no. I can't not get this," he mumbled to himself, rifling through the bag for what seemed like an eternity before his fingers finally found the cool thin metal of his mobile phone.

He pulled the phone from his bag and plucked the thin, raised button at the top of the device. The screen illuminated, and Danny instantly punched in a series of numbers which allowed the device to work for him and him alone.

"Dammit, come on!"

A menu of icons appeared on the screen, and Danny tapped the one resembling a camera. He turned the phone sideways and raised it in front of his eyes, finally bringing what remained of the creature into focus. He tapped the camera icon repeatedly, snapping picture after picture of what remained of the beast, which by this point in its re-entry wasn't much. The thing's entire body was submerged now, leaving only its head exposed, and from this distance and perspective, Danny could only capture it at an angle between the left ear (if it had ears at all) and the back of its skull.

He took several more shots, he had dozens at this point, but each one seemed worse and less convincing than the last, until finally the thing disappeared entirely beneath the surface. The last photo caught the top of its head; to an objective observer, the picture could have been anything from a stone to the head of a porpoise.

Danny put his hand to his forehead and stared at the ground, his eyes wide with disbelief. He tossed the phone into his backpack and then stood staring out at the ocean for another ten minutes, waiting and hoping for it to return. But he knew what he had seen was probably a once in a lifetime event. He suddenly had the thought that he'd forever be one of those Bigfoot spotters or UFO abductees that popped up from obscurity to tell their tales on basic cable conspiracy shows. Nobody ever really believed those people, of course, but by the end of those shows, Danny always left a little room for acceptance. Nothing was impossible, even urban legend stories, especially if they were rooted in scientific achievability.

And now he had a story of his own. His life would be different going forward. No matter how long he lived, nothing would ever be the same after today. *I'll be part of the crazy, conspiracy crowd*, he thought, one of the loons that normal people humor in the moment and then laugh about once that person has finally shuffled off, wide-eyed and irritated, mumbling something about the government.

But Danny could be different. Danny had pictures. Not great ones—he'd comb through them thoroughly once at home—but pictures nevertheless.

He stuffed his feet into his shoes and tied them tightly before descending the stairs that led to the beach access boardwalk. He left his towel on the sand and his clothes on the bench, and then nearly sprinted the 3.7 miles back to his house.

Chapter 2

"TAMMY!" DANNY BEGAN calling his wife's name before he even opened the door. "Tammy!"

He detected movement through the hallway, past the kitchen, outside on the back deck. He ran to the door and opened it with ferocity, causing Tammy to scream and nearly drop the bougainvillea she was in the process of hanging.

"Jesus, Danny! What's wrong with you?"

Danny leaned over, hands on his knees, catching his breath for the first time in twenty minutes. The sweat dripping from his head onto the wooden beams of the deck came in sheets.

"You need to take it easy on these runs, honey. You look like you're in the midst of a stroke."

Danny held up a hand, and pressed it out toward his wife, a motion telling her both to give him a moment to find oxygen, and not to leave his sight.

"What's wrong? You're scaring me. Did something happen? Why are you still wearing your bathing suit?"

Danny stood tall and took one more huge breath, glancing at his swimming trunks with vague curiosity. "Oh my god, Tammy," he said breathlessly. "Oh my god."

"Danny! What is *wrong*?"

"Nothing is wrong. I'm fine. But I have to tell you something. Show you something."

"Good lord! What? Are there aliens on the roof or something?"

Danny opened his eyes wide and cocked his head, indicating that Tammy wasn't as far off as the wildness of her remark implied.

Tammy furrowed her brow and smiled, giving a nervous giggle at the end.

Danny stood tall and put his hand on Tammy's back, ushering her inside to a seat at the breakfast nook table. "Don't move."

Danny ran to the foyer and got his backpack, fishing the phone from the front pocket and opening his photo gallery. For the first time since he made his mad dash from the beach, he looked at the pictures he'd taken and was immediately disappointed at the first of the images that appeared. He knew at the time they weren't great, and that he'd bungled the opportunity to get more of the ocean creature's full body, but he was hoping for something a bit better than these first two revealed. He was suddenly dismayed.

He swiped to the left, bringing up the next picture, which was grainier and worse than the first two. The fourth picture was the best of the four, and the remaining two dozen or so, those that showed only the submerging top of the creatures head, could have been anything: a hat floating on the surface, a dark basketball, even the head of a normal man wearing a swimming cap.

Danny walked back to the kitchenette and his awaiting wife, swiping and assessing the pictures over and over again en route. He shook his head the whole way, tears of disbelief forming in his eyes.

"Did you see Elvis?"

Danny looked up at Tammy, bringing himself back to the moment, suddenly noticing, as if for the first time, how stunningly beautiful his wife was. Danny smiled and calmed his emotions, and then stared down at his phone, swiping to the fourth picture in the series. This was by far the best one, but it was still a completely inadequate depiction of what he'd witnessed less than an hour earlier. "Look at this."

Tammy took the phone and stared down at it, and then held it up to eye level, squinting as she did. "What the hell is that?"

"I don't know—not exactly—but what I'm going to tell you is absolutely what I saw." Danny stared at his wife, waiting for confirmation that she would believe what he was about to tell her.

"Okay." Tammy flashed an intrigued grin.

About halfway through the recounting of events, Danny could tell that his wife, in fact, did not fully believe him. There was a frown at one point. A scrunching of confusion at another, as if the facts weren't lining up. But he soldiered on, getting every bit of detail out, trying to be as precise as possible.

"And you're sure it wasn't just a man?" Tammy finally asked after the yarn was fully spun. "It was still a little dark right? That time of the morning? And you said your eyes were blurry from the water."

"No. I...My eyes were blurry from the water when I first got out and saw the woman standing there. Not at this point. And does this look like a man?"

The phone was flat on the table now, and Tammy looked at the photo again, leaning in close, hands folded in front of her mouth, the posture of someone prepared to reassess with fresh, objective eyes.

"No, it doesn't. In all fairness it doesn't. But pictures play tricks, Danny."

Danny groaned. "I saw it! *You're* looking at the picture, but *I* saw it! That's what makes this the real thing. And I didn't see just the head. I saw the whole thing...its body! It was standing on the beach for Christ's sake!"

"Okay, I know, I'm sorry." Tammy paused. "But eyes play tricks too, Danny."

Danny scoffed and shook his head, a thick look of disappointment blanketing his face. "Fine," he said, and then stayed quiet, pouting now at his wife's resistance.

"Danny, I believe everything you've just told me. But you also want me to believe that what you saw, whatever is in this picture, is...what? A sea monster?"

Danny tried to keep his tone of voice relaxed. He knew the louder and more animated he got, the more it detracted from his credibility. *It shouldn't be that way with my wife,* he thought, but there it was. "I don't know. But I saw something. Something that doesn't line up with what I know about the rest of the world. And unless you can come up with something more than a generic explanation for what I saw..." Danny didn't finish the sentence, but instead frowned and flicked his hands into the air shoulder-high, indicating to Tammy there was nothing left to say.

Tammy took the cue and stayed quiet for a few beats, and then asked, "This woman that was there. Do you think she saw it?"

The woman. How had Danny not asked himself this question? Until now, he had thought of this morning as two separate events: the woman on the dunes, and the creature from the ocean. But Tammy was right. Maybe she *had* seen it. Maybe it had been there earlier and she was looking for it. That would have explained the look of concern or whatever it was. Danny had never seen the woman before, and wouldn't know how to go about finding her exactly, but she was no day-tripper, about that he was pretty certain. She was a local. Maybe she would be at the beach again later today. And even if she wasn't, there were only so many houses around that part of the strip, if he had to, he could knock on doors, canvass the area until he found her.

"She may have. That's interesting, I hadn't really thought about that, but she may have. I need to go back down there today anyway. I left my towel and clothes. Maybe she'll be there again."

"Or maybe...you'll see *it* again."

Danny shook his head. "If I see it, so will a hundred other people." Danny knew the beach would have started filling up by this hour, and in a couple more it would be packed.

"Well, good luck finding your stuff. Do you want me to come?"

Danny didn't. His marriage was one of the parts of his life that was fine, he guessed, but maybe wasn't working out perfectly. At least not in his mind. He wasn't sure whether Tammy felt the same, at least not in a conscious way that she would have admitted to. "No, it's fine. I'm just gonna drive, so I should be back in a few minutes."

"Okay, honey. Love you."

"Love you too," he said, and then slammed the door.

THE BEACH HAD INDEED filled up considerably by the time Danny arrived, evidenced by the fact that there were no general parking spaces available. Instead, he parked in one of the four handicap spaces that sat vacant, taunting him. It was an unDanny-like thing to do, but he felt different now, like mundane things such as parking laws were no longer applicable in his life.

He reached the top of the landing and saw that his clothes had disappeared from their spot on the bench, and didn't appear to have been scattered about anywhere else on the overlook. Less than ninety minutes since he'd left, and a pair of old shorts and a vintage Oasis tee shirt were now gone, likely stolen by some poorly-raised degenerate. Two minutes later, Danny was down on the beach discovering his towel too was nowhere to be found. That all of his belongings had vanished was certainly unusual; this wasn't the kind of place where petty crimes like linen burglary happened very often. He'd left all sorts of things at the beach before and almost always found them exactly where he'd left them. This clearly wasn't his day.

"Great," he murmured to himself, staring at the sand as he began to circle a blanket where a young couple had decided to set up camp for the day. They were early twenties, and Danny made the snap criticism that at least one of them should probably be on the way to work at this time of day, if not already there. At the very least they should be at school. It was a Thursday morning, a workday, the time for people under sixty-five to be productive; never mind that Danny, himself was also strolling the beach at this hour, and based on his own logic, at thirty-eight years old, should be at work too.

"Did you lose something, buddy?"

The man component of the lounging couple pulled his sunglasses to the end of his nose and squinted up at Danny, a wry smile on his lips indicating he'd had about enough of the middle-aged guy buzzing around his girlfriend, who, herself, lay unaffected by Danny, ostensibly asleep under a pair of Wayfarers.

"I did, as a matter of fact," Danny replied. "I was down here earlier today, just before dawn." This last bit of superfluous information sounded to Danny like some type of jab of superiority, though he wasn't sure he meant it that way. "I'm pretty sure I dropped my towel somewhere around here. You haven't seen it have you?"

The kid scoffed. "Nah, bro. Sorry." The kid repositioned his sunglasses to their rightful place and reclined back, once again completing the perfect pair of bodies next to his girl on the blanket.

"How about a sea monster? You seen one of those?" Danny had moved his attention from the couple now, and was lost again in the memory of his morning as he looked out toward the place in the ocean where the black creature had emerged less than two hours ago.

The kid laughed. "Nope. No monsters either."

"You sound like my aunt," the girl said, not moving a muscle other than those needed to speak.

Danny felt the sting of a chill on the back of his neck, and a small lump began forming at the bottom of his throat. He stepped around to the girl's side of the blanket. "Your aunt talks about sea monsters?"

"It was a joke, buddy," the guy said. "Come on, that's enough now. We don't have your towel. Leave us alone. Please."

On any other day it was a joke, Danny thought. But not today. "What did you mean by that?" Danny ignored the guy's command and moved closer to the girl, now squatting beside her.

"Hey!" The guy stood up and removed his glasses fully, tossing them to the blanket. He began shaking his hands and shoulders, loosening up, preparing for some type of barefoot beach combat.

Danny stood tall again and faced the guy, hands open and facing out, showing his lack of malice while simultaneously preparing his defense.

"Chill, Mark," the girl said finally, seeming to time her words just at the moment of the tension's crest. She sat up and pushed her Wayfarers to the top of her head. "It was meant as a *kind* of a joke, the thing about my aunt, but she *is* into that type of thing."

"'That type of thing,' like weird things? Or specifically what I said? About a sea monster?"

"Dude, what the hell are you talking about?" Mark asked, chuckling with sarcasm. He was now standing stiff, chest out, moving in on Danny, ready to throw down at a moment's notice.

"Mark! Enough!" The girl was done with Mark's macho routine, and shot him a look that made her words redundant, letting it linger on her boyfriend until he dropped his eyes to the sand and shook his head in a movement of both defeat and disgust.

"I don't know. She used to tell us stories when we were kids. Crazy stuff about creatures in the ocean, aliens in the sky, stuff like that. They were ghost stories, I know, but she always told them like they were real. Scared the shit out of me and my brothers. And the one about the sea monster—'The Ocean God' she called it—she told that one a lot. Always serious about it too. Never softening the details for the sake of sparing us kids. It was kind of bitchy, actually, now that I think about it."

"She lives here? Your aunt? This side of the barrier island?"

"Yep. We're staying at her place now. Mark and I just got here this morning. Her house is just over there." The girl pointed to her right, past the dunes where the woman Danny had seen that morning had been standing.

"Is she there now?"

The girl shook her head. "She said she'd be gone when we arrived. Which she was. I don't know if she left this morning or last night. In any case, she wasn't here when we got here." She snickered. "I love her and all, but I don't think I'd last more than a day at her place while she was there. She's crazier than monkey shit."

"She's got a fat place though!" Mark chimed in, holding a fist out for the girl to bump, which she did gleefully, her tongue out as she laughed at their luck for having a crazy, possibly wealthy aunt to take advantage of.

Danny stared blankly at the two, waiting for the joke to pass so he could get back to the conversation. The girl noted Danny's frown and her laughed trailed off. "What's your interest in my aunt anyway?"

Danny shook off the question, as if it wasn't the girl's right to ask it. "What does she look like?" Danny was pushing it now, but this was likely to be his only chance to speak with the girl, and he didn't want to leave clues on the table.

The girl grinned. "She's actually kind of hot. But isn't that a wedding ring I see on your finger?"

Danny looked at his wedding band, confused, and shook his head quickly, again dismissing the question. "Is she about my age, maybe a little older? Brown, shoulder-length hair?"

"Yeah, I guess," the girl replied, and now the irritation that Mark had felt earlier seemed to be seeping into his girlfriend. "But that describes, like, every woman I see over thirty."

Danny stayed silent for a few beats, processing all of the information he'd just received. There was no real evidence so far that the woman he'd seen that morning was this girl's aunt, and far less evidence that she knew anything about what he'd seen walk out of the ocean. But it wasn't impossible.

"Okay, thanks. I mean it. I'll leave you guys alone now." Danny nodded and turned away, but looked back suddenly, inquisitively. "One last thing: you wouldn't mind telling me your aunt's name, would you? Just in case I have some questions for her?" Danny flashed a coquettish smile, indicating to the girl that he may indeed have a romantic interest in her aunt after all.

"Questions?" Mark asked, "Who the hell are you? A detective? Can I see your badge, Detective Douchebag?"

Danny had 'Sorry, forget it' on the tip of his tongue when the girl, whom he now realized was also not attached to any name, decided to answer.

"Sure, why not? Her name is Lynn. Lynn Shields. Like I said, her house is right on the beach. Fifth house to the left after you leave the access."

"What the hell?" Mark asked, once again heating up. "Why don't you just give him a key to the house?"

"Oh relax. He seems cool. Maybe he can bring a little naughty excitement to Lynn. Lord knows she needs it." The girl winked at Danny, indicating that if those were Danny's intentions, his secret would be safe with her. "I don't think she's even gone on a date since Lyle died." The memory of whoever Lyle was seemed to immediately sober the girl. "Anyway, she's supposed to be back Sunday night, but I wouldn't chisel that into any stone tablet if I was you. She can be a little...erratic, I guess you'd say."

"Thank you, uh..." Danny left the gap purposely, hoping the girl would fill it with her name.

"Tracy. Tracy Amato"

"Trace!" Mark scolded.

"Oh, who cares?" Tracy dropped her glasses into place and lay back down, unconcerned.

"All right, happy?" Mark asked. "Now leave us the fuck alone. And I hope your fucking towel is half way to Portugal by now."

Danny smiled and nodded politely. "Thanks Mark. You have a nice rest of your day. Though shouldn't you be at work or something?" Danny didn't want to fight, but he couldn't help tossing in a light jab.

"I work in a hotel. Nights. What's your excuse, asshole?"

Danny looked off into the distance, sincerely pondering the question. "Before today I didn't have one. But I think I do now, Mark. I think I do now."

Chapter 3

"WHY DO WE HAVE TO LEAVE so early, Lynn? Since when are you such a morning person?" Lyle Bradford ruffled his hair and slipped on his flip-flops, yawning with half-open eyes.

"Just come on, whiney." Lynn Shields was frantic inside, but she was using every grain of concentration to stay composed and casual.

She grabbed her boyfriend's hand and led him out the door, striding into a fluttering jog, him flailing behind her as they made their way through the backyard to the overgrown path that led to the dunes.

By her estimation, she still had two weeks left—even now, after ten years, it wasn't an exact science—but after last cycle's failure, and the ensuing worst year of her life, she wasn't taking any chances.

Still, she'd fallen in love with Lyle, and had prayed all year that it would never come to this. She had even considered telling him about the God, considered bringing him into the fold, perhaps convincing him to help her secure the victims.

But Lynn always knew that Lyle Bradford was too kind to be a merchant of death. He didn't have those same qualities that she had. Was she a monster? Probably. At least, she understood, that most objective people would deem her as such, and she accepted that assessment as a real possibility. But this ability to lure and murder existed inside her nevertheless, monstrous or not, and she decided the inheritance of the ability contained its own value, and it was not for her to judge.

But Lyle was different. Lyle wouldn't have offered up a squirrel for sacrifice, let alone his fellow man. He was sweet, and his sweetness made him vulnerable, a perfect replacement plan for the one that collapsed only weeks ago.

It was a sound plan, the original, and one she'd worked on all year. Rove Beach was more upscale than most beach towns, but it had its share of homeless. Seven of her first nine victims, in fact, had been vagrants, men Lynn had befriended in secrecy on the streets in town and then lured to the beach in the middle of the night, rewarding them with cash and full bottles of whiskey. The rapport with the men wasn't easy, however, and always took months to build, so when her intended victim for this cycle was found dead on the beach from an overdose—at the very spot where the God would be arriving in less than six weeks—she was thrust into a full-fledged panic.

But this year she'd made a back-up plan. She didn't always have one, but after last year's heartbreak, she wasn't taking any chances. But that plan, too, became a pile of ashes when Lynn's sister—who was scheduled to visit with her kids and perpetually-cheating husband, the man Lynn had targeted for the sacrifice—had canceled her trip at the last minute.

At that point, she was left with few choices. One choice really. There had been no time to devise anything else, at least not one that was certain not to miss.

"I didn't bring a towel," Lyle pled, a last-ditch effort to forego this pre-dawn outing.

"It's fine. We're just gonna take a walk. Besides, we're a hundred yards from the house. If we get back and want to stay down here for a while, you can run back and get a couple of towels."

Lyle yawned. "Fine, but you're running back. I'm too tired."

"You won't be after the walk. Just stop talking for a second."

Lynn stood atop the dunes and stared off to the Atlantic, she far more fascinated by the water below than her lover of a little over a year. He appeared to be sleeping on his feet, wavering in the breeze.

Lynn was breathing heavily in anticipation, her heart pounding beneath her hooded windbreaker.

She had sent out the signal a little over an hour ago, only minutes after rising from bed like an assassin and walking to this very spot. Here she had lain the compact boombox in the tall grass and pressed the play button on the CD player.

The high-pitched siren had blared out toward the sea, the sound mixing seamlessly with the mating calls of the insects. Other than the awakening of a few dogs in the vicinity—at every other time of the year, Lynn saw dogs only occasionally, even on the beach—the siren song went undetected, even in the quiet of the predawn morning.

She had made the decision to let the recording play longer than usual this time, though being that this morning's try would be the first of the new cycle, her expectations weren't particularly high. But even if she was too early, she wanted to get Lyle in the habit of these morning walks.

They would be taking them every morning until she saw it.

"Let's go," she whispered, and stepped slowly down the dunes, Lyle wiping the sleep from his eyes as he trailed behind her.

Chapter 4

LYNN SHIELDS WAS NOT a name Danny recognized, but, in all honesty, there was no reason he would have. Rove Beach wasn't that kind of place, one where everyone knew everyone else. For being adjacent to the ocean, it certainly didn't have that beach town charm one normally expects from a city as small and quaintly located as the one in which they'd chosen to live. At least for a while. Tammy had once suggested the motto of the place should be "The small town with the assholeness of a big city." Danny didn't go quite that far, but her point was taken. People kept to themselves here. There weren't a lot of 'Good mornings' or tips of the cap when you passed people on the sidewalk or on your way out of a store. To this point, almost ten months since Danny and Tammy had moved in, they had made no real friends. They'd never gone to lunch with another couple or even been invited to dinner. Of course, he and Tammy had made no bona fide attempts to fit in either, which, Danny concluded, was probably why they picked Rove Beach in the first place. They were the same type of people.

Danny sat tall in his office chair, tickling the keyboard as he thought how best to query. Just start, he thought, and then he typed the woman's name into the long, thin search engine box, along with the name of the town. No reason to over think it.

He scanned the first page of results and saw one that looked promising. It was an online article from the Beach Rover, the local paper, the one he'd been toying with the idea of subscribing to, but that he'd ultimately decided to pass on, fearing that reading the paper every day would turn him into an old fuddy-duddy.

But there it was, the good old internet, presenting the name Lynn Shields, bolded in black in the midst of a paragraph which, based on the truncated text of the search engine copy, indicated it was part of an article about some type of tragedy of which she was a part.

He clicked the link and an article appeared titled "Search Continues for Man Missing from Rove Beach." The article was dated October 22, 2007.

The search continues for Lyle Bradford, a local chemist who is thought to have been swept from a sandbar along the 700 block of Atlantic Drive. Police arrived at the scene at approximately 6:20 am, Sunday morning, after responding to a call of a possible drowning. Bradford's girlfriend Lynn Shields called police after losing...

"Danny?" It was Tammy.

"Hey."

"Watcha doing?"

"Just uh...a little research." Danny continued staring at the screen without reading, hoping to send the message that he was busy.

"Did you find it?"

Danny turned to Tammy. "It?"

"Your towel, right? Isn't that what you went back to look for." Tammy rolled her eyes and snorted a laugh. "Did you think I meant the Creature from the Rove Beach Lagoon?"

The thought of striking his wife had never crossed Danny's mind, but at that moment, just for a beat, he felt a real desire to stand up and slap her. Instead he held his tongue and emptied his thoughts, focusing on the moment and not his mind. "I didn't find the towel, no. Anything else?"

Tammy cocked her head and frowned apologetically. "Oh stop it, I'm just kidding. I told you I'm open to believing what you saw. Let me see the pictures again."

"Forget it."

"Come on."

Danny started to feel like a child, like a little boy being picked on by his bully big sister. He decided not to respond.

"Did you find the woman at the beach?"

Maybe, Danny thought. "No."

Tammy lingered behind him for a few moments—Danny could feel her thinking of something to say, something that would give her reason to stay—and then the sound of footsteps clicked back to the kitchen.

As was often the case around this time of day—with the morning routine over but before the lunch hour had arrived—Tammy was bored. It was one of the unintended consequences of their windfall. She had quit her job as an elementary school vice principle when they moved, and, since she and Danny had no kids of their own, she hadn't yet found that thing to occupy her newfound free time. At least once a month, Danny would encourage her to go get a job, anything, even if it was as a substitute teacher or office assistant, something that would get her out of the house and engaged in the world. It wasn't that Danny was sick of his wife—not really—he just knew that in the long run, Tammy being busy and stimulated would make for a much happier household.

But she always stalled, telling him at first that she just wanted to take three months, then six, and then it was a year. Danny was going to hold her to this latest time line, since a year seemed like a real benchmark. In another five or six weeks, he was going to insist she start looking for something to do.

Danny was often bored too, of course, but he technically had a job. Songwriter. It was a bit preposterous, he thought, seeing as he hadn't written a single lyric in over eighteen months, but he was just taking some time. Just another six months, and then he'd start working. Ha!

Bradford's girlfriend, Lynn Shields, called police after losing sight of Bradford early yesterday morning. The report stated Bradford had swum on his own to a sandbar of the coast, and that Shields saw several waves sweep over the sandbar just before he went missing.

It is not clear why Bradford swam to the sandbar. Foul play is not suspected.

This last line struck Danny as odd. Foul play? Of course foul play wouldn't be suspected. Why would this question even have been asked of investigators to begin with?

Danny checked the byline at the top of the page. Sarah Needler. He wrote the name on the first buck slip in a thick pad of buck slips he kept on his desk—ostensibly for that occasion when the muse arrived and he was struck by a verse of pure genius—and underlined the name twice. The search to uncover his mystery sighting had begun.

THE WOMAN CHECKED HER watch and then looked back to the path that led to the beach access. He was a few minutes late today, but if her timings were accurate, he should be coming any time now, turning the corner with that quick sprinter's burst, straight down the path that leads to the access and then up the stairs to the overlook. Same as yesterday. Same as the day before that. It was the same routine, six days a week for the last three months, when she first began the search for her newest offering in a long line of sacrifices.

The woman checked her watch again and then the skies above, as if her assessment of the creeping sunlight was a more reliable device than her timepiece. He was late today, the runner, at this point just a little, only a few minutes, but in this practice, a few minutes was everything.

The timing had to be perfect.

Yesterday it wasn't. The God hadn't come when it was summoned. That wasn't altogether unusual, not on the first attempt—in fact, the first few tries almost always failed—but next week would be different. She always made adjustments, just as she would this time. There were still almost two weeks left in the cycle, plenty of time. But none of it was available to waste. She had to get it just right.

What she couldn't do was miss it. She couldn't wait another fourteen months. That was simply impossible.

Except that it wasn't.

She had missed the feeding once before—only once—and that year had been, without a close second, the most tortuous of her life. The pain had been crushing, almost completely debilitating, and as she thought of it now, her eyes watered with fear at the possibility. She pressed her lids with the tips of her fingers, and the fear slowly dissolved, seeming to chemically change within her, now forming a light film of regret.

Regret about the year that followed.

She had killed the only man she ever loved, had sent him to his death, as surely as any judge who had ever sent a convicted man to the gallows. She'd never made any attempts to rationalize her actions, nor did she try to diminish the anguish he no doubt suffered. As it did for all of them, Lyle's death appeared to be excruciating.

She held the shame and guilt in her mind for several moments, focusing on it, living it over now as she sat alone on a wooden bench just outside Rove Beach Park. She never pretended to be justified in what she had done, and the pain she experienced that morning, all those years ago, still lingered today. But that was a pain she could live with.

The other type, the one that had enveloped her when she'd missed the sighting—the feeding—she could not.

And here she was again, engrossed in another cycle, each of which became more difficult than the last. The offerings went quickly once the God took them, but keeping the feedings secret, and for her eyes alone, was a task that required meticulousness. As was true of most of the towns in this part of the country, particularly those on the coast, Rove Beach grew in population every year. And the diversity of the immigrants that flocked here made the feeding schedule that much more complex. Retirees and students, bums and exercise nuts, early risers and nightgoers, all combined to make the whole affair increasingly problematic.

But she'd been watching for months now, measuring, timing, and she had found one day, one spell during the week along the precise stretch of beach where the God emerged, when there was never a soul. Except for one.

The runner.

Yesterday was the first try and she'd failed. Miserably. Not only did the God not arrive to her summons—which was, again, not all that unusual—but the man had seen her! So lost was she in concentration, staring with concern at the place where the God emerged every year and two months, awakening for a few weeks to find its food before submerging again to its chamber of water and muck, that she never noticed the runner's arrival. He must have been camouflaged by the darkness of the water when she'd arrived, beneath the waves, or perhaps had slipped back onto the beach under the cape of night. How could she have been so careless as to not do a proper surveillance, particularly on the first attempt?

But in truth, that the runner had seen her was unimportant. He knew far less about her than she did him. She didn't know his name, but she knew he was new to Rove, and that he had no real acquaintances to speak of, at least as far as she could tell.

Besides, what was notable about her standing on the dunes that would make him remember her, even if they crossed paths again? A woman such as herself staring at the ocean on a seasonally warm morning was as common as the waves themselves.

Still, she had to do better. It was her first call of the season, yes, but she'd still executed it very poorly. She should have been hidden near the beach, watching him as he finished his morning swim, weapon in hand, waiting until the creature either emerged at dawn or not.

But she'd gotten lost again in the anticipation, so obsessed was she with the ocean beast.

Thankfully, the God hadn't answered her. The calculations she had made over the last two decades had narrowed the window for her slightly, and she'd become more precise with the arrival, but there was work to do still.

Two decades. She was only in her forties. Almost half of her life had been devoted to these few weeks, every fourteen months, during which only a few moments of those weeks were filled with the spectacle on which she subsisted.

The devouring was a miracle.

The woman closed her eyes and groaned at the feeling the memories of the feeding produced. The power of the creature, so docile-looking and benign just before the event, and then terrible and primal when the instinct finally arrived.

What if it had come after she fled?

The thought shot into her mind as if sent from somewhere deep in the earth, and terror suddenly flooded her brain. What if she had made a grave miscalculation? Waited long enough that the signal was received, but not long enough to see it emerge? Perhaps it had fed already! This last thought brought tears to the woman's eyes, and suddenly she couldn't breathe. The man wasn't arriving today because he was already dead! The event had occurred! Had she checked the paper today? One day probably wasn't soon enough for a drowning or missing person to have made it into the paper, not without a witness seeing him go in. Still, there had to be another way to find out.

Lynn Shields thought back to the day Lyle died, and could recount virtually every word she'd told to the police. And to the reporter after.

As she drifted unwillingly into this memory, she heard the huffing of a man, mouth open and working. It was the runner. He was later than he'd been the day before. She looked at her watch again and added it to the calculus. She'd made no calling to the God today, and she prayed it wouldn't come anyway.

Today was for surveillance. She had to get better.

Chapter 5

EVEN AFTER THE EVENTS of yesterday, Danny kept his morning routine as usual, just as he'd done for over nine months now. He finished off his stair climb atop the overlook and checked his watch, noting that he'd arrived a few minutes later than normal. *It's a miracle I'm here at all,* he thought. Nobody would have blamed him for taking a day off.

But here he was again, at the beach, sticking to the dream, though the swimming part of the habit wouldn't be happening today. And probably never again. Certainly not in this ocean. Not unless Danny got some very satisfactory answers to the questions he had about what had erupted from the water the day before.

He kept his clothes and shoes on and walked to the bottom of the overlook on the beach side, and then sat on the second to bottom step, staring off toward the section of the water where his sighting had occurred. Every wave looked like a head in the darkness. Every lap on the shoreline sounded like the eruption he'd heard just before its arrival.

Danny sat there for several minutes until the sun rose above the horizon and the first of the beachgoers arrived, an elderly couple who Danny thought he vaguely recognized. It was Friday. If the weather held, the beach would be crowded by nine.

Danny nodded to the couple and jogged back up the stairs and headed towards home. The creature hadn't come today, and he had a phone call to make.

"HELLO?" THE WOMAN ON the other end of the line answered on the first ring, her voice gruff and hurried. Danny was caught off guard, and for a moment considered hanging up.

"May I please speak with Sarah Needler?"

"Speaking."

Sarah Needler no longer worked full time for the Rover, but according to the news desk at the paper, she still freelanced on occasion, though it had been almost a year since her last story was published. But they had a phone number for her and were, at least in Danny's opinion, a little too willing to give it out. He expected the number to be old or out of service.

"Hi Ms. Needler, my name is Danny Lynch. I was wondering if I could ask you a question or two about a story you wrote several years ago."

There was no reply on the other end, and Danny realized he hadn't asked a question. Must be a reporter thing, he thought. They were probably used to people keeping their thoughts to themselves and not speaking unless queried directly.

"Would that be okay?"

"I can't stop you from asking the questions. Whether or not I answer them only time will tell."

Danny had now formed an image of the woman, and it wasn't what he'd expected. She sounded older than he'd calculated—mid to late sixties—with a heavy dose of something New York and Jewish.

"You know I don't work for that paper anymore, right?"

"Yes, ma'am. And I'm sorry to track you down like this."

"Honey, all I've done for the last forty years is track people down and ask them questions. So a piece of advice: once you've got 'em on the line, don't waste time with apologies. Now what've you got for me?"

Danny got to the point. "In 2007 you covered a story about a drowning. And I realize that drownings probably aren't all that unusual here, and it was a long time ago, but I thought you might..."

"Bradford. Lyle Bradford."

Danny's body chilled at his shoulders. "Why do you remember that?" And then, as if the words were spoken by some inner force, he added. "Or are you just one of those people who remembers everything?"

Sarah laughed long and fully, chuckling a few more times at the end before trailing off into a fit of long-time-smoker cough. "I remember the names of my grandchildren, everyone I voted for for president, and the date my brother died. Other than that, it's a crap shoot. But I remember the drowning of Lyle Bradford."

"Okay, but, if I may ask: why? Was there something unusual about it?"

There was a recollecting pause on the line. "I don't suppose it was anything that would have held up in the Court of the Unusual, it was just a hunch really. I'm old enough to remember when people relied on those. Anyway, I had a hunch about the girlfriend, that's all. She was lying. The story she told to me was a lie."

The story Danny read had no quotes from Lynn Shields, or anyone else for that matter, but he saved that fact for later. "How can you be sure?"

"It's a clichéd answer, Danny, especially coming from a reporter, but I'm going to give it to you anyway." Danny liked that she remembered his name. He liked this woman instinctively. "In my business, people lie to you all the time. And after a while, you get very good at being able to tell the difference between a lie and a truth."

"Do you have any idea *why* she would have lied?"

There was silence on the other end that lasted almost ten seconds.

"Ms. Needler?"

"Can you talk in person, Danny?"

"Sure, of course, whenever."

"How about in an hour. Reefside Bar on Archimedes. I'll be on a stool at the end."

"I'll be there."

"And Danny," the woman said, "call me Sarah."

SARAH WAS INDEED AT the end of the bar, and Danny noted that his phone-call-based image of the woman wasn't that far off. She was thinner than he'd expected, maybe a few years younger looking, but the attitude and years he'd pictured in his mind were all over her face.

"Sarah?"

The woman continued staring straight to the bar back as she exhaled a long plume of cigarette smoke. She crushed out the butt and looked at the stool beside her, patting it once in invitation.

"It's nice to meet you," Danny said, maneuvering his way between the seat and the bar. "Thanks for meeting me."

"I invited you." Sarah replied.

"Yes, but...anyway."

"Do you want a drink?"

It was 11:30 in the morning, but the bar was open, so why not? "Sure." Danny nodded toward the bartender. "When you can, I'll have that IPA." He pointed toward the end tap which was adorned with wheat stalks and citrus fruit.

The bartender spun a pint glass from the cooler and tipped the faucet handle toward himself. He filled the glass to the brim and then laid a cocktail napkin in front of Danny and the glass on top.

"Thanks." Danny sipped the head and then picked up the glass, taking in a full swallow.

"Better?" Sarah asked.

Danny grinned. "Do I seem on edge?"

"You look like you've got something on your mind. Something more than your condolences about a guy you never met who drowned ten years ago."

Danny let the words settle, but he didn't take the bait. He pivoted back to the phone call. "So this woman, this Lyle guy's girlfriend who you said lied to you back in 2007, I met her niece on the beach yesterday."

"Is that why we're talking? You met the niece of someone who dated a guy I wrote a story about during the Bush administration?"

"No, I..." Danny trailed off, irritated with himself for not collecting his thoughts better before this meeting, for not having a clear strategy on navigating the current conversation. The woman beside him was sharp; charm and bullshit weren't going to get him far. He took another sip of his beer.

"Look Danny, you can keep to yourself whatever secret you're hiding. I'm not going to press you on anything. Just ask me whatever you want about her. Lynn Shields, right? That's who you want to know about?"

Danny took out his phone and looked at it for a moment, and then laid it on the bar top, staring at it for another beat.

"Is there something you want to show me?"

The woman was observant, that was for sure. "Maybe. But not yet."

Sarah gave an understanding nod and took a long sip of what appeared to Danny to be a gimlet.

"Why did you want to meet me in person? What was so important that you couldn't tell me on the phone?"

Sarah looked at Danny for the first time, her brow furrowed. "Nothing. I just wanted a drink."

Danny smiled weakly and shook his head once, as if he'd been duped.

"And I don't like to drink alone. Though I will if I have to." The woman dropped Danny's eyes and paused, and then said, "You wanted to know why I remember the Lyle Bradford drowning?"

"Yes."

Sarah was hunched forward, bracketing her drink with her elbows, her chin above the cocktail glass, staring forward. "I went to visit her the day after the drowning," she said. "The police had closed the case, and I'd already written the facts of the story for the column and it was ready for print. Truthfully, there was nothing particularly strange about the tragedy. But, and I guess if I weren't a re-porter I'd be ashamed to say this—but I am, so I'm not—it had been a pretty slow month in local news. This is a quiet town, so Slow is the name of the game typically, but that month was particularly brutal. We're talking, how-much-the-Corkers-netted-at-their-yard-sale kind of slow."

Danny laughed out loud, the beer presenting the first signs of its effect.

"So when the drowning happened, and I had plenty of time on my hands, I asked my editor if he would hold the story for another day so I could maybe try to get a little something more out of it."

"Like an interview with the bereaved?" Danny wasn't judging, just ac-knowledging that he was following along.

"An interview with a witness," Sarah corrected without an ounce of coyness. "I wasn't looking for blood, just more depth to the story."

"I didn't mean..."

Sarah waved off Danny's introduction to an apology. "Anyway, my editor agreed, so I jumped on it. I got the address where Lynn and Lyle lived—well, where she lived alone after that day—and I headed toward the story. But before I went to see this Lynn Shields person, to ask her if she'd be willing to talk with me, I decided to go to the spot on the beach where the tragedy happened, just to try to get a better picture of the Where and How of the whole thing."

"Is that standard?"

Sarah shrugged. "Not really. But I figured whatever story I'd end up writing would have something to do, at least in part, with how Rove needed to increase safety at the beaches. Adding lifeguard stands or flotation device stations. I don't know, I was just trying to get a feel for the place to inspire the direction of the piece."

"I didn't see any interview in the piece you wrote."

"That's because it was never published." Sarah guzzled the last of her drink and held the glass up, flicking her head once toward the bartender. "You gotta let me finish talking, Danny, or I'm going to be too sloshed to get to the end."

Danny tipped his head deferentially, holding up his IPA to indicate he'd let her go on. He didn't want to come across as being too eager or prosecutorial, but he was gripped by the story, and he was hoping that whatever had prevented Sarah Needler from writing that follow-up story had something to do with the thing he'd seen at the beach yesterday.

"I went there, to the beach, right to the spot where Bradford had supposedly drowned. It was a miserable day. Rainy and cold. Even the heartiest of beachgoers weren't coming out on that day. The whole week had been like that if I recall."

The bartender gracefully slid another gimlet between Sarah's arms and then pointed at Danny's empty beer glass with eyebrows raised, expertly asking if he needed another, careful not to interrupt the conversation. *Two beers before noon?* Danny thought. *On a Friday? Technically a weekday, but not really. What the hell?* he decided, and then gave an assertive nod, lips pursed, as if the refill should go without asking.

"Atta boy," Sarah said, obviously noting Danny's internal conflict. "Anyway, she was there. On the beach. Right on the water's edge near the spot where the drowning had evidently taken place. I had never seen the woman before, but I knew instantly it was her. Wind and rain be damned."

"That makes sense though, right? Her boyfriend drowned at that spot the day before. I wouldn't think it all that unusual for someone to mourn that way. Even in bad weather."

"Not at all," Sarah agreed. "It was my first reaction too. So I stood there on the overlook watching her and I felt really sorry for her. And honestly, if she had just been standing there, or even sitting in the sand watching the waves crash up onto the shore, crying and screaming at the water, I'd have thought nothing at all of it. Other than sympathy, of course."

"So there was more?" Danny obviously knew there was, but he wanted to lead Sarah to the point.

Sarah looked up at Danny and frowned, a look of irritation at the superfluousness of the question. "I started down the steps to the beach, to get closer, to make sure I was seeing things correctly." She paused. "And I was. The woman was on her knees, her arms raised straight above her head, and she was leaning forward toward the water and then back up straight. Over and over she did this. It must have been a dozen times."

"She was bowing? Bowing to the ocean?"

"Right. Exactly. Bowing. The way someone begging for mercy at the foot of some medieval king might do."

Danny let this information process, feeling unsettled by the second. But he continued playing the pragmatist. "I guess I could maybe see that. Not knowing her religious leanings, I could imagine someone who was grieving making that kind of gesture. Some form of prayer maybe."

Sarah smiled up at Danny. "You'd make a good reporter, sport. You've got a knack for skepticism."

Danny blushed foolishly at the compliment.

"And you're right; I considered the exact same thing as I walked down those steps and on to the sand. I kept my eyes on her the whole time. I was riveted. Like I said though, it was cold and rainy that day, and I was downwind from her, so she never heard me coming. If I had been calling her name the entire way she wouldn't have heard me. The wind was that strong. But as I got nearer to her, I could start to hear her." Sarah stopped and took another swallow of her drink, teasing the story just right.

Danny let the silence do its work and waited for her to continue.

"She was laughing." Sarah nodded at her own words, as if she needed to hear this part of the story aloud to be convinced of its accuracy. "But I know what your skeptical mind is thinking, Danny boy; you're thinking that laughing isn't so unusual either after a tragedy, right? You hear about people laughing hysterically at funerals or whatever, as some kind of built-in emotional barrier?"

Danny hadn't formed an opinion on the laughter yet, but now that Sarah mentioned it, it made sense.

"But it wasn't like that. This laughter was...gleeful. Joyous. But also..." Sarah stopped, as if her years of writing only the facts were preventing her from too much editorializing about the nature of Lynn Shields' laughter.

"Also what?" Danny prodded.

Sarah looked at Danny and shrugged. "'Maniacal,' I guess is the word. 'Demented' maybe."

Danny felt a chill, but hid it. "So what did you do?"

"I'm a reporter, and I still wanted the interview, so I kept moving in closer. And as I did, I could hear that she was also shouting out some barrage of words between the laughter. From where I was, I couldn't understand what she was saying, so I kept moving closer, hoping to at least gather a little of the content before she knew I was there."

"For what reason though? Did you suspect her of something at that point? Did you think she was confessing or something?" Danny immediately thought his question sounded a bit too aggressive, like he was accusing Sarah of being some type of spy or voyeur.

Sarah thought for a moment and then furrowed her brow and nodded. "You know, I'd never really thought about it that way, but I think that might have been it."

"And did you hear anything like that? A confession?"

"Only when I was a few feet away could I really understand the words, and it was only the last part of a sentence I caught before she noticed I was there. But this is the weird thing: when she did notice, she didn't look at me right away. She didn't turn toward me at all, made no physical gesture that indicated she'd detected me, other than that she stopped bowing. That's weird right?"

It was, Danny thought, but that went without saying.

"But I knew *she* knew I was there, because she suddenly got real quiet and still, and I was close enough to her now that I could see a calm smile form along the side of her face. And it was that smile that, you know, in the context of the words I had heard, terrified me."

"What...what did she say?"

Sarah looked up at Danny and frowned. "I heard nine words, Danny, and I have no idea what they meant. But they scared the shit out of me."

Danny waited, his breath held.

'There's always more. I can always give you more.'"

Danny kept a straight face, trying to stay sensible and non-judgemental, but the truth was the words scared the shit out of him too.

"So are you ready to tell me your story yet, Dan, or should I just keep talking?"

Danny had to make an on-the-spot decision: he could show his semi-conclusive photos of the thing he now suspected was responsible for the death of Lyle Bradford, or he could extract more from Sarah, get the full scoop about Lynn Shields, and then investigate the rest himself.

"There's not really any secret story," he lied, choosing the latter of his two options. "Like I said, I met Lynn Shields' niece on the beach today and she made the woman sound very interesting. So I did a little research on her and found your story about the drowning."

"So why are we having this conversation then, Danny?"

Danny paused. "Okay, listen," he started, speaking in a way designed to give the impression that he was ready to give up his ruse. "There was a line in your piece. It said, 'Foul play is not suspected.' It jarred me a bit. Like you were implying there was some reason that foul play could have been a possibility. It just intrigued me, that's all."

"And you call every reporter who writes something you find intriguing?"

"Only about seventy-five percent of them."

Sarah gave a doubtful smile, and Danny knew she didn't believe any of what he'd told her regarding his motives for contacting her. It was true, of course, that he was intrigued by the line, but he was also leaving out the main component of his tale.

"So you talked to her then?" Danny asked. "After she saw you there?"

"I told her who I was and asked her if she wouldn't mind answering a few questions for my story."

"And she agreed?"

Sarah nodded. "But not after doing a whole metamorphosis out of her hypnotic delight into something a bit more appropriate for the circumstances. She never acknowledged what I saw and heard right before she noticed I was there, but there was an understanding between us. An understanding that whatever she told me from that point on wasn't going to be the whole truth."

"But you interviewed her anyway."

Sarah shrugged. "I had to give her the benefit of the doubt. Maybe she could have convinced me that it all went down the way it did in the police report, and that whatever she was doing on the beach that morning was strange, yes, but not an implication of her complicity. Or maybe she would breakdown and confess."

"I'm guessing none of those things happened?"

Sarah shook her head and looked off to a space on the ceiling, pondering. "She was lying to me. I knew it the second her story started. I recognized some of the same words and phrases she told to the police, words and phrases that don't come the same way twice. Lyle Bradford may have drowned on that beach back in '07, but it didn't happen the way Lynn Shields says it did. Honestly though, I could have printed her interview anyway—it's not really important whether the person is lying, as long as I don't lie about what they've said. But I couldn't do it. I just told my editor she wouldn't talk."

Danny gave the woman a somber nod, knowing that her decision not to run any further with the story was due to her decency. Sarah Needler could live with someone's lies being accurately printed, but not when they involved the loss of an innocent life.

"Have there been other unusual deaths around here in the past?" Danny thought it best to get off Lynn Shields for the moment. He cut the air with his hand when the bartender motioned him for a reset, thus starting the process of bringing the whole meeting to an end.

"Drowning isn't all that unusual in a beach town. Especially in an ocean front town like Rove. Riptides and rough seas claim people all the time. Add in alcohol and out of towners, people who don't know the waters or even how to swim sometimes, and you'll get your share of drownings."

That made sense to Danny. The ocean had been swallowing people up for as long as there'd been people. And now sitting at this bar on a Friday afternoon, two beers in, he, for the first time, wondered on how many occasions the ocean had been used to cover a murder. Was it in the thousands? Hundreds of thousands? And what was the connection between the woman he saw—whom he still didn't know for sure was Lynn Shields, though he was going on that assumption—and the creature he'd seen on the beach? After hearing Sarah's story, he was convinced there was definitely some tie between the two. Based on the prayer motions Sarah had described, maybe the woman even worshipped the thing. He had to find her. He had to find someone who could explain to him what he'd seen. It was now the only thing in his life he could imagine doing.

"How was the trip?"

Danny shook his head and looked at Sarah. "Huh?"

"Looks like you just traveled off somewhere. And somewhere far by the looks of it."

"I...I have to go," Danny said softly and threw a twenty on the bar. "Thanks...again...for meeting me."

"I told you..."

"I know, *you* asked *me*. But thanks anyway." Danny walked toward the door and then stopped and turned back to the bar. "Sarah?"

Sarah cocked her head a quarter turn toward Danny's voice. "Yo."

"That piece of yours that I read on the internet, that was the original piece?"

"Uh huh."

"Why did you mention the part about not suspecting foul play? Before you ever even met Lynn Shields."

Danny could see Sarah cock her head to the side, a motion that acknowledged the question was a good one. "Reporters have hunches sometimes, Danny. Like I said. I guess I just had a hunch after reading the drowning report. One that told me there might have been more to the story. It was a good one I guess."

Danny paused. "A hunch, huh?"

"You got it, Danny boy?"

Danny waited at the door for a few more beats, waiting to see if the reporter had anything else to add. "See you around, Sarah Needler," he said finally, and then walked out the door.

Chapter 6

LYNN GAVE A DISCREET peek at her watch and abruptly stopped walking, turning sharply toward the water and the horizon beyond. The sun would be rising soon and they would need to head back. The arrival spot was not negotiable; it could be any day now. "Let's just take it in for a moment," she said, sighing with content, "and then we'll head back."

"Take what in?" Lyle snickered. "The sun has another twenty minutes at least." He was playful in his response, Lynn thought, and had seemed to warm to the early walk after only a few minutes.

"I love the ocean at this hour." Lynn wasn't sure she had ever mentioned this intimate piece of information to Lyle previously, but there it was.

"Since when?"

"Since forever. I just have a hard time getting up." Lynn flashed her eyes up at Lyle, batting her lids once for effect. "But I want to start. This week. And I want you to come with me."

Lyle frowned down at Lynn, his eyes narrow and doubting. "Oh yeah?"

"Yeah."

"You discovering religion or something?"

Lynn let out an anxious chuckle, and she covered her mouth in embarrassment.

"What's going on with you, Lynnie?"

She was still smiling, thinking about how close Lyle had been with his guess. Of course, the reason behind her newfound love of morning beach strolls wasn't religion *exactly*, but there was some resemblance to it. "Nothing baby. I'm just thinking about happy things."

Chapter 7

DANNY RECOGNIZED THE woman to his right immediately. He had always been good with faces anyway, but in this case, he had no doubt about who she was. It was the woman he'd seen on the dunes a couple of mornings ago, the woman he now believed to be Lynn Shields.

He slowed his pace as he reached the corners of Fromme and Pickering, a lightly trafficked intersection at which he normally never broke stride. But he was extra careful today, coming almost to a stop as he gave one slow glance to his right in an ostensible check for oncoming cars.

The woman in the Cadillac adjusted her sunglasses and turned away, then looked at her watch and took a sip of her coffee, pretending not to notice Danny in the slightest. But he knew the profile from the dunes, and the same look of worry.

He was on his way home from the beach. It was only the fourth day since Danny had seen the creature, and, almost inconceivably, he'd already begun to doubt what he'd witnessed. Four days. Even with the ambiguous photos, which he still stared at several times a day, the memory was becoming elusive, like a dream that seems destined to change your outlook on life forever the few minutes after you wake, but which somehow fades into oblivion by the middle of the day.

Danny had to fight against his instinct to run to the car, to knock on the window and ask the woman if she had a few moments to speak with him. This was his chance to see if she was, in fact, Lynn Shields, and if she had any connection to the beast on the beach.

But Danny's restraint won over, and, after only a second or two, he recognized the obvious: it was no coincidence that the woman from the beach four days ago was on this street at this hour, just as he was passing by. She was watching him.

Danny had played back his conversation with Sarah several times in his mind, and specifically the words she had heard Lynn Shields say on the beach that morning following her boyfriend's death.

There's always more. I can always give you more.

These two sentences, in combination with the accompanying prayer motions, left little doubt in Danny's mind that Lynn Shields had offered up her boyfriend as some kind of sacrifice. It was almost obvious.

And now, for the first time since he'd drawn that conclusion, he had another thought: What if Lyle Bradford wasn't the only one? What if there had been others before him? And after him? And as Danny followed this thinking further down the line, he now considered that the reason he was being followed was because he was on the woman's short list of possible future victims. He was at the beach alone almost every day. He was the perfect target.

As he did on every one of his running days, Danny crossed the intersection at Fromme and Pickering and ducked through the passageway of hedges that led to a sidewalk a half mile from home. Here he stopped and waited. He was out of the view of Lynn Shields now, so if she was indeed following him, monitoring his schedule, in just a few moments she'd drive off.

Danny pushed back through the hedges and walked again up to the corner of the two streets. The Cadillac was gone.

Danny walked to the spot where the car had been parked and started down the street toward the home Lynn Shields' niece had pointed out to him. But then he thought better of it. If she was following him, and if she did know something about the creature he'd seen on the beach, he didn't want to spook her. He'd let things play out a little further. The time didn't seem quite right. But it would be soon.

Chapter 8

"I WANT TO GO WITH YOU today."

Tammy was sitting at the table in the breakfast nook, her shoulders high and eager. She was donned in a raspberry-colored running suit and her hair was tied back tight in a ponytail. Danny thought she looked great.

"I feel bad about the other morning, about what you saw and the way I was...well, making fun of you. I would be mad too."

Danny wasn't mad, not anymore, but he understood why Tammy would have thought so. He'd barely talked to her since that morning, since his discovery of Lynn Shields and the follow-up details that were provided by Sarah Needler.

"If you don't want me to go..." Tammy stood up and frowned, and then walked to the kitchen counter where she began fussing with an invisible mess, making a show that she was hurt by Danny's hesitation.

"No...no, it's fine." It wasn't entirely fine, especially considering his new belief that he was being stalked. But he was stuck, unprepared for an excuse about why she couldn't come along. "I'm not ready yet, though." It was only 5:30 in the morning; he couldn't remember the last time he'd seen Tammy up before 7:00, barring some travel day.

Danny ate a light breakfast of blueberries and toast, put on his long, nylon running pants and a tee shirt, and within ten minutes, he and Tammy were out the door and en route to Rove Beach.

"So now that a few days have passed, do you have any more theories about what you think you saw?" Tammy smiled and shook her head. "What you *saw*, I mean?"

Most of the catharsis that Danny gained through his morning runs came from the quiet and solitude they provided. He didn't mind the company—Tammy was his wife, after all, and he was glad that she had shown some initiative with her exercise—but he wasn't going to be game for chatting the entire time. Especially not about a topic that had become as heavy and gnawing as the sighting. As it was, he had to slow his pace to about half just to stay close to her; he'd have to drop it to three quarters if she intended to have full on conversations about serious events. "No, not really. I don't know what it was."

"Of course, but what do you think?"

"The more I think about it, the more I think you might have been right," he lied. "It was dark. Maybe it was just a man. Some big guy in a wet suit or something. He would have had to have been enormous, I'll admit that, but I suppose it's not impossible. And maybe he had a snorkel that I couldn't see, and that's how he just disappeared back into the water."

Danny hadn't actually ever thought about any of this as a possibility—the words were just coming from him, creatively, like a child inventing a story to stay out of trouble. But as he said them, he started to frame the picture in his mind, comparing it to what he had actually seen. Or thought he saw. Was something like what he'd just described to his wife a possibility? Maybe Lynn Shields and Lyle Bradford and Sarah Needler all had nothing to do with what he'd seen, and he'd just filled in the gaps of the story that didn't make sense with his own narrative. Or, perhaps, they were connected somehow, but in a way that was more scientifically explainable, even if still nefarious.

"But...you said you saw it. Is that what you saw? A man in a wet suit?"

"Jesus, Tammy, what do you want me to say?" Danny stopped suddenly on the path, allowing Tammy to pass him a few steps before she stopped as well. "A few days ago you thought I was delusional, and now—"

"I never said you were delusional. That's not fair."

Danny closed his eyes and scoffed, shaking his head slowly; it was a motion that let Tammy know he was wrong to go against his instincts and should have maintained the regular privacy of his morning routine. He said nothing more on the subject, and began his run again, this time at his normal pace, which had become quite fast over the last nine months. Tammy followed in silence, but she lasted only twenty yards or so before Danny pulled well ahead of her, out of the range of conversation.

Twenty-five minutes later Danny reached the path side landing and ascended the staircase to the overlook, where he waited at the top for his wife to arrive. Another fifteen minutes passed before Tammy finally appeared, hands on her hips and gasping, her lungs well past capacity as she climbed the stairs in a slow, plodding walk.

"Thanks for waiting," Tammy said in the middle of huffs, the phrase sounding to Danny simultaneously grateful and sarcastic. She sat on one of the benches and wiped the sweat from her face with a towel, continuing to catch her breath. "You must have been very worried."

"I knew you'd make it. I'm actually impressed. Three and a half miles is not a joke if you're not used to running it."

Tammy gave a thumbs up, still working hard to steady her breathing. "You're not going to swim are you? That water must be damn cold."

"It's always cold at 6:30, but trust me, it's warmer out here than yesterday. Anyway, it doesn't matter, I don't swim anymore. My daily-dip-in-the-ocean days are over."

"Really? I didn't know that. Since when?"

Danny looked at his wife and frowned, clicking his eyebrows up, giving her a chance to reach the answer on her own.

Tammy mouthed a silent "Ohhh" in understanding. "I guess that makes sense. I wouldn't swim in sea-monster-infested waters either."

Danny chuckled at this and started down the steps to the beach. He stood alone on the sand for several minutes, staring toward the area of the ocean that had bred the creature. He closed his eyes and tried to remember it all exactly, recreating it in his mind, and then his mind went to the woman, Lynn Shields, and he wondered if she was watching him now.

Danny turned back toward the overlook where he could see the outline of Tammy, standing meditatively in the pre-dawn morning, leaning against the railing and staring out over the water. "Do you want to see where it was?" he said "Do you want to see where it happened?"

Tammy was broken from her spell and nodded with apparent excitement, walking quickly down the wooden planks that formed the access staircase. When she reached the beach side landing, she looked across the beach and said, "Man, it's dark out here."

Danny took this statement as a subtle inquiry, that she was indirectly asking Danny how it was possible he could be sure about what he'd seen last week in this visibility. He argued the point in his head on two counts: first, he *wasn't* sure about it; and second, the sun had risen. Tammy had seen the pictures. It was still a bit dark when he first heard the sound in the water and the thing started to walk out, but by the time he'd run back up to the top of the overlook and grabbed his phone, there was a decent amount of sunlight. He said none of this to his wife, of course, knowing that she would have interpreted his unsolicited explanation as defensiveness, what she would have called 'projecting.'

"How far away were you when you saw it?"

"I was here." Danny walked back to the second step from the beach landing.

"And where was the...whatever?"

Danny didn't have a good landmark to choose from, since the beach was void of any lifeguard chairs or benches. But he could line up roughly where the thing came out by the houses that rose up beyond the dunes. He looked at the one Tracy had pointed out to him, the one belonging to Lynn Shields, and then grabbed Tammy's hand and guided her to the approximate spot in the sand. He then turned back toward the staircase they'd just descended. From this distance, at this time of morning, it was virtually invisible, and now that he'd paced it off, he may have gone a bit too far. But not much. This was about right, he thought. "About here."

"Here? Really?"

"Yeah, I think so. Why?"

"I...I don't know. It just seems kind of far. How could you have seen something that was here from the beach steps?"

"The sun had come up, Tammy. You see how it's almost up now." Danny's snappy voice was emerging. "You know you can see better when the sun is out, right? I mean you saw the pictures. It was light out." There goes keeping the peace.

"All right, all right, no need to get nasty. You need to be able to answer these questions."

Danny frowned, mostly out of disappointment in himself for allowing Tammy's doubt to upset him. The truth was she was right: her skepticism was probably a good thing. If he, himself, was going to believe what he'd seen, he needed to be able to answer these questions in his own head. It probably wasn't a great sign for his relationship that his wife wasn't a little more supportive, but that was another topic entirely.

Tammy walked towards the water, her chin up, head slightly cocked to the side.

"I think we should probably stay away from the shoreline, Tammy. You know, just in case I'm *not* a basket case."

"What is that noise?" Tammy asked. "Do you hear that? It's like a buzzing noise or something."

"Really, Tammy?"

"What?"

"'A buzzing noise?' Like 'zzzzz?' That's insects. They're pretty common at the beach at night, in case you hadn't noticed. The sound is from cicadas, I think?"

"Cicadas buzz during the day. The night sounds you're talking about are crickets and katydids."

Tammy had minored in Entomology at the University of Maryland, so Danny had little to come back at her with in terms of a rebuttal. "Fine. Crickets and crazydids then."

"Katydids. And that's not the sound I'm talking about. It's lower pitched than that. And not as constant. It comes and goes. You don't hear it?"

Tammy's voice was coming from different places, and with dawn still a few minutes away, she had strayed beyond where Danny could see her. She now sounded like she was up toward the dunes. "I don't know, maybe. Where are you?"

"It almost sounds like a whale call." Tammy was now to Danny's left again, back down by the shoreline, trying to chase down the sound.

"I thought those calls were like foghorns. Almost so low that people can't even hear them."

"That's true for the bigger whales—blue whales, humpbacks—but not all of them."

"What do you know about fish anyway? I thought you were a bug expert."

"First of all, I'm not an expert. Second, whales are mammals, and third, you have to take a lot of zoology classes when you study entomology, and you tend to remember a few things. Anyway, I'm not saying it *is* a whale, I'm just saying..."

Sploosh!

"What was that?" Tammy's voice was whispery, filled with fascination.

Danny could now see his wife standing with her toes in the water, the light of dawn breaking quickly now. "Tammy..." His voice was barely audible, even to himself, fear having choked the volume from his voice. He swallowed and focused. "Tammy!"

The top arc of the sun had poked through the horizon, and the first of the sun's rays draped across the ocean like yellow ice. Danny could see Tammy staring east toward the rise, simultaneously taking in the majesty of nature while searching for the source of the sound. "It probably is a whale, Danny!" Tammy replied. She was gleeful, dismissive of whatever alarm she may have detected in her husband's voice. "I told you!"

"Tammy! Now!" Danny paused, settling his emotions. "Let's. Go." He said the last two words slowly and sternly but without urgency, hoping that if his screams didn't encourage his wife, a solemn command might.

Tammy turned away from the water and Danny could see only the outlined silhouette of her. He couldn't see the expression on her face, but he knew it was one of irritation.

And then the expression became fear as she detected the creature rise up behind her.

And then pain as it opened its mouth wide and bit down into the side of her neck.

"TAMMY!"

Danny's feet slid out from beneath him as he tried to run toward his wife, and he fell flat to his chest, sand sticking to his lips and splashing into his eyes. He got up and tried to run again, but on this second attempt, as he lifted his right leg in preparation to dash toward the shoreline and his screaming wife, he felt a piercing pain as something sliced across his upper calf.

Danny fell back again to the same prostrate position, the sand in his eyes now mixed with tears of pain and despair, forming a muddy, blurred vision of the scene in front of him.

The creature, the one he'd seen less than a week ago and had grown to doubt its existence since then, had his wife's head gripped between its hands. Its fingers were thick and long and covered Tammy's ears and cheeks, holding her in a way as if about to crush her face. The bite it had taken removed the entire right side of her neck; had the creature simply released Tammy's head now, it would have flopped over to her shoulder in a dead heap.

Danny silently prayed she was dead, but he detected a look in her eyes, a look of disbelief that penetrated her paralysis, conveying agony and sorrow. She looks like she's apologizing, Danny thought, but for what he couldn't have described.

He tried to rise again, but the muscles in the lower part of his right leg were no longer responding to his brain's commands. He stayed focused on Tammy, not allowing himself to think yet about what had caused his own injury. Using what strength remained in his upper body, Danny pushed himself up so that he was standing on his left leg, and he began to hop toward the shore line and the massacre unfolding there. With every small leap he got closer to the creature, and as its looming body approached, so too did the smell of death and rot.

Danny knew he was as dead as his wife now, there was no question in his mind about that, but he would keep moving forward. There would be no attempt to flee without at least trying to bring peace to his dying wife.

He was less than five feet from the scene now, having made his way to the tip of the tide's reach and the ground beneath the monster. The muscles in his left leg were exhausted of energy and Danny collapsed to the wet sand; he was now sitting with his legs splayed out before him, as if enjoying the soft feel of the waves as they broke quietly on the shore. He looked up and saw the blood spewing from between his wife's shoulders, and the bits of flesh and hair hanging from the creature's mouth. Its eyes were menacing, crazed, but its only focus was on the flesh it was eating. The sun was halfway over the horizon now, but the animal was still too dark for Danny to make out any real distinguishing characteristics.

Except for its teeth, which rose up and down, machine-like, destroying any bone or skin or muscle that passed between them.

Danny vomited twice and then got to his knees, the blood on the back of his leg warm and stinging, now caked with salt and sand. For the first time, he looked away from his wife, and considered now what had caused the wound to his leg. He turned and looked behind him and saw her, a woman walking slowly, cautiously, never once looking at Danny, all the time gawking at the scene playing out behind him.

It was the woman he'd seen on the dunes, and yesterday in the car, the woman he'd decided was Lynn Shields. And she was laughing, crazed in her fits, all the while tears streaming her face. In her hands she gripped a long wooden pole, the top of which was adorned with a large blade that rose above her shoulders, its shape thin and curved like the head of a vulture. She was the perfect manifestation of Death, Danny thought, carrying the literal weapon of the Grim Reaper himself.

Danny turned his head back to the shoreline and the creature. It had now torn one of Tammy's arms from her torso, and his wife looked almost doll-like in appearance, as there wasn't much more blood for her to lose. She was gone, dead, her suffering finally ended. It was Danny's turn to sacrifice himself now, and he bowed his head in some type of honor gesture, waiting for the inevitable.

But the inevitable never came, and as he knelt there with his head bowed for what must have been at least two minutes, he thought about the moments of his life that had brought him to this place.

Danny lifted his head finally and stared back at the creature. It had turned away from him, east toward the sea, beginning its walk back into the surf.

Danny thought again of that morning only days ago, when he had watched it make the same watery march. This time, however, one of its hands was gripping the exposed spine of Tammy Lynch, dragging what remained of her torso behind it.

Danny watched in a combination of terror and disbelief, first feeling the need to scream, and then, more practically, to try to get to his feet and make his way back to the road for help. Danny wasn't sure about the extent of his injury, so running may have been impossible anyway, but he wouldn't have run if he could. He was unable to look away from the creature, mesmerized by its power and ferocity. Did anything on earth come close to it?

Danny heard movement behind him and turned back to see the woman with the scythe. She was less than five feet from him now. She stood tall and rigid, her focus still locked on the creature as it descended back to the ocean. She was sobbing now, holding her hands out wide, embracing the world, the scythe in one hand like a wizard with a staff attempting to conjure the gods.

Still on his knees, Danny turned back to the water again and watched the last of the creature enter the water, its black head sinking like a tree stump beneath the now-blue ocean. He covered his face with his hands and leaned forward into the sand and began to sob.

"No!" Danny screamed, but his mouth was dry and hoarse, and the sound was swallowed by the wind that began whipping across the beach. There was no fear left in Danny; the terror was now completely replaced by loss and awe.

He turned back to the woman again, and this time felt the butt end of the scythe land squarely between his eyes.

Chapter 9

SARAH LOOKED AT HER list of unread emails, and when she saw the paper clip attachment symbol next to the first one in her inbox, she nearly deleted it on the spot. She was no sucker, and she wasn't about to expose herself to the latest boutique virus that had been pitched out to the unsuspecting world.

But then she made the connection. **dlynchmob70@gmail.com.**

dlynch. That was Danny, and the time stamp on the email showed it was sent the previous night at 12:04 am. Sarah opened the email and read:

Hi Sarah—

Thanks for meeting me the other day. I wasn't sharing everything with you, you know that, but I wanted to meet you first before I showed my hand. So here it is: I had a sighting. I saw something that I don't think is known to exist in this world—at least not by anyone outside of this town. Look at the pictures that I've attached and tell me what you think. Feel free to share them, but I'll tell you now, the picture doesn't do justice to what I saw. If, after looking at it, you want to hear more from me, I'd love to tell you the whole story.

Also, I think what I saw has to do with the Lyle Bradford drowning. Call me. 221-483-3387.

—Danny

Sarah swallowed hard and looked at the attachments at the bottom of the screen, and then clicked on the first one and downloaded it to her computer. The image sprung forward, and she knew almost instantly that Danny was right. The thing in the water—and she admitted to herself she had no idea what it was—had something to do with the drowning of Lyle Bradford. She recognized the perspective immediately, and thought back to the day she'd come up behind Lynn Shields on the beach, at just about the point where Danny's 'sighting' was in the water.

Sarah opened the other four attachments and looked at them, and then printed them out on her color printer, not that the color was going to make much of a difference in deciphering what the thing was. She felt a familiar tingle in her belly, and imagined it was time to start writing again. To start reporting again.

Sarah dialed Danny's number and got his voice mail. "I saw the pictures," she said, "and I'm in, Danny. I want to know all about what you saw. Call me back."

She then dialed the direct line of Tom Strap, managing editor at The Rover.

One ring. "Strap speaking."

"I've got a potential story for you, Tom."

"Nice to hear from you Sarah."

Sarah was both impressed and flattered that Tom recognized her voice instantly. "Remember Lyle Bradford?"

Tom laughed.

"I'll take that as a yes. Give me a day or two, but I might have a story like you've never seen."

Chapter 10

"HOW MUCH LONGER ARE we going to do this, Lynn? Really, I like that you want to spend so much time together, and get all this exercise, but why does it have to be so early?"

"It's been five days, Lyle. Jesus Christ, fucking forget it then."

"Hey, hey! Where's all this coming from? I'd just like to sleep in once in a while."

"Fine. I heard you. I said forget it. I'll go alone."

Lynn was taking a gamble with this strategy, but she had always known there was a chance it could come this, her playing the role of the distraught girlfriend who just wants to be loved by her boyfriend, the jerk refusing to reciprocate.

"What's going on, Lynn?" Lyle was serious now, the concern in his voice obvious. This somber, adult state was a rare one for him to be in. "You've been as edgy as I've ever seen you. And I feel like these walks are making it worse. Ever since we started, you've been agitated all day."

This was all true. There was still a week left in the cycle, maybe ten days by Lynn's calculations. It was plenty of time, and she could feel that it would be coming any day now, but what if it didn't? What if she hadn't missed it last year at all? What if it just hadn't come and was never coming again? At some point it was going to die, just like every other creature on Earth. Lynn began to sweat, and she felt herself on the verge of hyperventilating as these thoughts fired like missiles in her brain.

"I'm just going to go."

Lynn walked up the dunes and past the radio, which was shrouded in sea grass and darkness. It was 5:03 am, and the recording of the minke whales had been playing on a loop for a little over two hours now. On top of the stress that always accompanied these few weeks every fourteen months, there was also the fact that Lynn got almost no sleep.

She walked out to the beach and then down to the north pier, a distance of about a mile and a quarter, where she turned around and started back toward home. There was no point in the walks without Lyle, but she had to follow through with her bluff. If she simply stopped and crawled back in bed, she would miss it. Her chance at seeing it this cycle would be lost. No, she had to see it through, play out the role to the best of her ability.

There was, of course, always the chance that the God could emerge now, while she was alone, in which case she wasn't sure exactly what would happen. She could scream for Lyle, she supposed, and then use the blade on him as he ran towards her.

Lynn turned and headed back toward home, and as she did she felt for the handle of the knife behind her, sighing deeply at the feel of the hard rubber handle, knowing that the steel, business end of the weapon was sheathed comfortably below it. The knife in this form was not her typical weapon of choice. The one she had constructed to shepherd the offerings over the years was much more cumbersome, the long, bladed pole a bit unwieldy at first touch. But that weapon gave her the luxury of distance, and, with practice, she had grown quite adept with it. She'd had to use it only a few times in actual practice, of course, as most of the men she'd lured had been unconscious when the God arrived and her assistance would have been redundant.

Lyle would be different though. Harder in more ways than one.

Lynn looked up and saw the silhouette of her house and headed towards it.

"Lynn." Lyle was standing in Lynn's path, the darkness still making him invisible from ten feet away.

Lynn caught a scream in her throat and stopped walking. "Lyle, what the fuck?" she said, still acting out the scorned woman act.

"Sorry. I was going to catch up with you if you had just waited, but then I didn't know which direction you went. So I just waited here."

"Waited here for what?"

Lyle walked forward so that Lynn could now see him, and grabbed her arm gently, leading her with him down to the water's edge.

"What is going on, Lyle?"

Lyle reached his left hand into the pocket of his khaki shorts and pulled out a small rounded object, and then dropped to one knee, opening the clamshell case as he brought it up to the height of Lynn's waist.

Lynn swallowed; the tears that had welled were already falling to the sand at her feet. She was unable to speak.

"I love you, Lynnie," Lyle began, his voice as unsteady as the hand holding the ring case. "And I want to spend every day with you for the rest of my life. So...if you feel the same way, will you marry me?"

Lynn put her hands to her mouth and began sobbing, the shame that was the true source of her weeping disguised by the overwhelming emotion that was known to accompany such events as a proposal of marriage.

"Lynn?" Lyle giggled at her reaction. "It's okay, baby." He stood now, facing his assumed bride to be. "It's okay. I love you and I..."

The sound of the splash was immense, and this time Lynn screamed.

"What the hell made that?" Lyle asked, staring out toward the water.

Lynn began moving backward toward the dunes. "Come on, Lyle. Now! Come on!"

"Hold on, baby. I bet it's some kind of whale or something. Did you hear that splash?"

"No! Lyle! Come on."

"Lynn!" Lyle shouted. He lowered his voice and said sternly, "Stop."

Lynn did stop, and she watched eagerly as Lyle walked alone into the surf, moving his head back and forth, surveying the water for the source of the sound.

She didn't see the first strike against the man who, had she been given another few seconds, would have been Lynn's fiancé. It was still too dark and Lyle had moved too far from the shore. She pulled the flashlight from her fanny pack and moved in on the sounds being made by her dying lover. She shone it straight in the creatures face, its black eyes dilating, making the hideous beast look even more amazing.

Lynn kept the beam straight and sat down slowly in the sand, her eyes wide, a long smile draped across her face, taking in the sight that had been her addiction for a decade now.

The creature.

She'd missed it last year, but not again. Not ever again.

"Lynn! Help me! Jesus Christ!"

Lynn Shields felt the sting of tears again, but cleared them quickly, angry that they were attempting to rob her of even one second of this miracle. She felt grief for Lyle, and at her life that was destined to be consumed by this addiction, alone in the sand, every fourteen months, waiting for a creature to emerge and destroy, and then descend back to the depths of the ocean. The whole thing—from the first splash to its descent back to the ocean—lasted less than six minutes. And she was already longing for the next cycle.

Chapter 11

DANNY AWOKE TO THE sound of crackling, and he opened his eyes to find a small fire burning off to his right, illuminating a small cave that seemed at first glance to be manmade, a small opening in the dirt that had been hollowed out and reinforced with a skeleton of wooden beams.

He was sitting against one of the cave walls with his hands low, tied separately on either side of his body to one of the boards that ran along the wall behind him near his lower back. His arms and body formed the shape of the letter M. He could see that the ground below him was a mixture of sand, dirt and sea grass, and that it had been bloodstained brown from the wound in his leg.

His eyes were also caked with blood, presumably from the blow that had been delivered to the middle of his head, and a bandana was laced through his mouth and was tied tightly around the back of his head.

The memory of Tammy came to him within seconds, and Danny gagged a silent scream, trying audibly to chase away the mental picture of the creature killing and decapitating his wife and then dragging her body to the endlessness of the ocean.

But the memory of the slaughter lingered, and he began to feel a vague comfort from it.

Danny cried softly, fighting the thoughts of the creature feeding on his wife, trying desperately to remember a time when she was alive and vibrant. He finally settled into a peaceful memory of Tammy on their wedding day. She was beautiful and glowing that Saturday in April.

Danny allowed himself a few more moments of these reflections, and then he re-focused, assessing his surroundings while trying to work out how he ended up there. Was there anything about the woman that could help him escape from this bunkered prison? And where was he exactly? He could smell the ocean and hear what sounded like the screams of children and bursts of laughter.

He initially concluded that the woman who had hit him must have had help to bring him here, otherwise, how else could she have moved him, unconscious, to the place he was now? Unless he was so close to the spot of his assault that she'd only needed to drag him the shortest of distances. This last theory started to seem like the right one, as it coincided with what he could see, hear, and smell.

Danny studied the fire for a few moments and noticed that, although it was burning inside of this cave, it seemed to be venting nicely, the flame pulling up towards the earthen roof and the smoke disappearing to the world beyond it. It probably had a few more hours at best, and then it would need to be re-kindled.

With this collection of clues, it didn't take long for Danny to put the pieces together and draw a conclusion about his situation: this place was not only his prison, it was a holding cell, the place where Lynn Shields kept her victims before feeding them to the beast of the Atlantic. It was a beachfront dungeon, one adorned with a bonfire and coastal sounds instead of hanging skeletons and screams of torture, but a dungeon nevertheless.

But escapable, Danny thought. It had to be.

He knew he wasn't very far from freedom, otherwise there would have been no need for the gag. And if he could hear the sounds of people coming from outside the cave, it reasoned that they would have the ability to hear him; though it was certainly a possibility that his muffled screams might barely penetrate the walls, only to dissipate into the sea air.

Danny looked to his left, following the corona of light formed by the fire, and saw a path of sand and dirt leading away from him, glowing out to a distance of about twenty feet or so, tapering off into a cul-de-sac of what appeared to be a narrow tunnel. The dead end of the short runway was shrouded in darkness, but through the last reaches of the fire's light, Danny thought he could see grass growing up and around it, sticking wildly out at various places on the walls and ceiling, vaguely forming the shape of doorway. That was the exit.

For the first time since waking, he tested the restraints of his bound hands, tugging on the ropes lightly at first, and then with all of his force. He pushed his back against the dirt wall and pulled his arms outward, feeling the burn of his shoulders and biceps. It was useless. He had no leverage to give any real challenge to the knots of the ropes, and even if he did, Danny didn't think it would have made much difference.

Panic was beginning to set in, and suddenly Danny's mouth felt as dry as the sand beneath him. His tongue was being pushed back by the bandana, clumping up against his windpipe, and it seemed to be swelling by the second as the moisture was sucked away by the cloth restraint. Danny shook his head wildly now, tears of desperation forming in his eyes as he considered that he might be in the initial stages of suffocation.

Relax.

He closed his eyes and bowed his head forward, and then lifted it, focusing his eyes on the dancing flame before him. *Stay here, Dan. This is where you are now, so stay here. You're not dying. You are a prisoner, but you're not dying.*

WHEN HE AWOKE AGAIN, the fire was out and the cave was completely dark. The sounds from outside were gone, and Danny could only hear the drone of cicadas from somewhere in the heavens. Or crickets, he reminded himself, and katydids.

The memory of Tammy entered his mind again, but the overwhelming grief of her death had passed, and this time Danny smiled through the gag, imagining he must have looked a bit deranged with his teeth bared that way. He was tending toward delirium now, he thought, and his thirst was maddening. It had been a full day he calculated. A full twenty-four hours since he'd seen the thing that had butchered his wife and the woman who sliced his leg and smashed his forehead. And he'd not had a drink of water since a few hours before that. And without the fire burning, the only thing Danny contemplated now was whether he would die of thirst or exposure.

He leaned back against the wall and craned his neck up slightly toward the cave ceiling, a movement that was half attempt to get as comfortable as possible before dying, and half prayer. Danny had recently labeled himself a spiritual atheist—whatever that was—but he was open to a full religious conversion now, and as he looked down the tunnel that led to the grassy arch and saw the glow of light shining through, so bright it was blinding, he thought perhaps this last ditch effort at religion had paid off. Maybe he was going to the afterlife after all.

Suddenly, the light dipped slightly and Danny could now see the outline of a figure moving towards him, crawling beneath the low ceiling of the tunnel, arms stretched out in front, crablike in its walk. It was human, Danny assumed, though after the week he'd had, that detail was certainly no longer a given. In one hand the being held a flashlight, and in the other a long staff with an immense blade on the end of it.

The figure was now only feet from Danny, and he could tell by the weapon that it was the woman. As she reached him, she dropped the scythe to the sand and reached out to him, her fingers shaped in a claw, grasping. Danny tried to scream, but the gag and aridness of his mouth produced nothing audible.

She reached toward his face, and Danny braced himself for the suffering that was certain to follow. But instead of touching him, she reached between his mouth and gripped the gag, maneuvering it past his chin and down to his neck, thus freeing his tongue and lips for the first time in what felt like a week. He gasped for breath, sticking his tongue out straight, stretching it, feeling the air like a serpent.

"You must be thirsty."

The woman was now kneeling in front of Danny, but he could only see the bottom half of her, the light of the flashlight not reaching her torso or beyond.

"And cold, I would imagine."

Danny began to whimper softly at the woman's first statement, simultaneously moved almost to tears by the idea of water, and distraught at the notion that the woman may only be torturing him with the possibility.

The gag was gone, but the lack of saliva in his mouth still prevented Danny from speaking, so instead he simply nodded once, squeezing back any tears that threatened to fall.

The woman had brought with her two large bags, the straps of which were slung across her shoulders, crisscrossing her chest in the middle between her breasts. The satchel portions rested on the ground on either side of her. From one bag, Danny could see large pieces of wood sticking out high in every direction.

The woman reached into one of the bags and brought out a full bottle of Dasani water, and then twisted to the left, snapping the cap free of the safety seal. It was the most glorious sound Danny had ever heard in his life.

"Open up."

Danny lifted his chin high and opened his brittle, sticky lips as if about to take communion.

"Swirl it in your mouth first," the woman said, pouring in a small amount of the warm water. "You have to get some lubrication in there or it will spill out."

Danny ignored the advice and swallowed the water immediately, tipping his head back to let gravity bring it into his body, careful to keep his lips closed so he wouldn't lose a drop. Once it was down, he moved his mouth back to position, silently beckoning for more of it. Beckoning for all of it.

The woman continued giving Danny small sips until the bottle was about a quarter full. "I know the thirst you feel," she said finally, twisting the cap back on. "I feel it every year. All year."

Danny blinked twice at the closed bottle, desperate for more. He couldn't see the top half of the woman, but he shifted his gaze toward where the woman's face would be, and considered for the first time since her arrival something other than his thirst.

"But you've seen it too now. The miracle. You're the first I've ever known—besides myself—to have witnessed it. Some of the sacrifices too have seen it, I suppose, the ones who were conscious upon its arrival. But they had only seconds to bask in it."

"That was..." Danny coughed, the dryness of his throat still resisting him despite the majestic relief the water had brought. But he fought through it. "...my wife. That was my wife."

The woman set the flashlight down flat on the ground now, and Danny could only see her feet as she shuffled over in the direction of the fire. He heard the sound of wood being unloaded, and within a minute, a new flame had sprung to life, and heat was returning to the cave.

The fire illuminated the room, and Danny could now see the glow of the woman's face. It was the same one he'd seen on the beach only days ago, yet the concern and angst were gone. There was only peace there now. Contentment.

"It was to be you," she said. "Not your wife. You were the one destined for this cycle."

Danny sensed dismay in the woman's voice, but he knew it was more to do with the failure of her plan than the fact that it was Tammy and not he who was taken by the thing.

"It was only fate that brought me here—to the beach—at just the time that he emerged. Otherwise I would have missed it again. It is just more proof that my God is so."

Danny noted the 'here' in the woman's sentence, and was now convinced that he was indeed at the place of the sighting, though he couldn't have said where exactly. And although he wanted to stay focused on his escape, the questions about all of this—this creature that he had seen on the beach last Thursday and that had now mauled and killed his wife—were overwhelming. "What is it?"

The woman smiled. "Going for the big question right off the bat, huh?"

Danny said nothing, his eyes narrowed and unblinking.

"I can only tell you the origins as I know them for me. That is as close as I can get."

Danny nodded.

"I was twenty-five when I saw it for the first time. It was the year my parents were killed. Traffic accident. A delivery driver for a beer company fell asleep at the wheel and smashed into their Buick head on. I was in graduate school at the time, studying to be a teacher—high school science—but after a hefty inheritance and an even larger settlement from the insurance company, I wasn't going to have to work again. So I didn't. My sister took the main house, but I had always wanted to live at the beach, so I moved here. Started living a life of leisure I guess you could say."

Danny closed his eyes as he listened to the story, thankful for the heat of the fire and the moisture in his mouth. His stomach rumbled just at the moment of Lynn Shield's pause.

"Of course," she said, and reached into her bag, bringing out a granola bar and a small container of almonds. "I'd intended to give this to you immediately."

She fed Danny the food, laying the almonds in her palm and raising them to his mouth like she was feeding a goat, and then followed it up with a few more sips of water. Afterwards, the woman laid a blanket across her prisoner's shoulders. She'd no intention of letting him leave, Danny thought, and it was a very likely possibility that she was saving him for the next round of sacrifices. But if that was to be his finale, at least he had these moments until the end.

"Back then, when it was warm enough, I used to sleep outside on a cot out on the dunes—that's where you are now by the way, underneath the dunes. You're only steps from the beach as the crab crawls. In any case, I had started taking up the practice of listening to sleep sounds on my radio. I had a tape that would play on a loop to drown out the buzzing of the insects, which was a sound that was always a little bit discomforting to me. There's something too high-pitched in the whirring that never relaxed me. Some people like the cicadas, but not me."

Danny considered correcting the woman, but thought better of it.

"And then one morning, just before dawn, I woke to the crash." The woman stopped for a beat and stared off into the fire, and then focused back on her prisoner, her eyes gleaming. "It was the one you must have heard this morning?"

Danny nodded.

"I knew that it had come from the ocean, the sound—where else, right?—so I walked down the dunes to the beach, down the path that leads right from my house. And I saw it immediately. It was still dark, so I could only see the outline. But I..."

The woman began breathing heavily, and a grin streamed across her face as she shook her head slowly, as if still not able to believe what she saw that first night.

"It was just...standing there, staring up towards me. At first I thought it was a man—some person in a frog suit or costume or something—but then it moved. It was slight, the movement, just a turn of its body toward me, but I knew instantly it was no man. It was something else. Something new."

There was another pause as the woman reflected on that first encounter, trying to summon up the feelings again, but, undoubtedly, falling short.

"I couldn't figure out what it wanted or why it was there, but it seemed to be expecting something. Something from me."

"Why?"

"Why what?"

"Why was it expecting something from you? Why did it come out at all? It just happened to be at the spot on the beach where you were sleeping?"

"Yes, of course. That was the question, right? I thought the same thing. And, like you, I didn't know at first."

The woman was getting excited now, her speech increasing as she recounted the events, including the feelings she had had about them as they unfolded at the time.

"I thought it may just have been a coincidence, that this creature appeared here randomly, accidently stumbling in front of my home. Me just as likely as anyone else, right?"

The woman nodded at Danny, waiting for a reply. Danny shook his head once and shrugged. "Right."

"But something deeper inside of me told me that wasn't right. It wasn't there randomly. It had come for a reason, and I was determined to find out what it was. So the next night, I repeated the same thing I had done that night before. And it returned the next morning."

She stopped again, forcing Danny to follow up. "Why?" he asked finally. "What did it want?"

The woman gave a wry smile, her eyebrows raised as if the answer was so obvious she shouldn't have to explain it. "It was the sounds. It was lured by the sleep sounds I was using to fall asleep."

The woman was smiling genuinely now, pleased by the cleverness she'd had and her power of deduction.

"So you can call this thing whenever you want? Just by putting on those sounds outside?" Danny was keeping to the facts, showing no signs that he was impressed by the woman's discovery.

The woman scoffed, seemingly irritated by the simplicity of the question. "Not whenever I want. No! After that second morning, it...it didn't come again. I called for it."

The woman was pleading with Danny now, her eyes expressing to him that it hadn't been her lack of effort that was the reason for its nonattendance.

"And I continued calling for it, playing the sounds every night. It came once more that cycle, a few mornings later, but then never again that year."

"So... then how did you know it was the sounds? Maybe the sounds had nothing to do with it at all."

"It was to do with it!" The woman almost growled her rebuttal, spittle flying from her mouth. She wiped her lips and chin, composing herself, and then placed another log on the fire. "The next time it came was over a year later. Fourteen months to be exact. I had played that sound every night without fail for the entire time—never once missing a night—and then it appeared again, just before dawn, fourteen months later, just as it was that first time, standing and staring up at me. It was like it had been waiting for me. But then, just as before, it walked off, back into the ocean. I...felt like...I was dying. I would have offered up myself to it to keep it from leaving again."

Danny ignored this last part, knowing this level of desperation was probably more than the woman had intended to reveal. He stuck again to the story. "How is it that no one else has seen this thing? Aside from you?"

"Oh, plenty have seen it, for centuries. All you have to do is spend a little time on the internet and you can find dozens of writings about it. Why it made itself known to them, I don't have any idea, but I do know the reason that I saw it, the reason it came to me. And it was by pure chance. As I said, it was drawn to the sounds that I happened to be playing those nights when I first moved in. I later learned that the sounds on those tapes were made by the mating calls of the minke whale. The God has an affinity for minke whales, perhaps; it could be its source of food, its sustenance during the rest of the cycle, during the times when it's ocean bound. Or perhaps it hears the same sounds as it ascends the shores in some other part of the globe, some place where minke whale calls come from the shore line, just as they do at my house."

Danny stayed quiet, staring at the woman. "The God?"

The woman ignored the clarifying question from Danny and continued. "So that was when I figured it out. It wasn't coming because it enjoyed the sounds. The God was coming for more than that."

"It was looking for food."

Lynn smiled and nodded, impressed by the quick understanding of her prisoner. "That's right. It was looking for food. And it then became my obligation to supply it with some. And from that night on, every fourteen months, that's what I've done."

Danny almost became sick to his stomach at this last phrase, but he was determined to keep the meager rations of the granola bar and almonds inside of him. "People?" It was all he could manage to say, but the message was received.

Lynn Shields stared at Danny for several seconds, silently studying his face. Finally, she said, "Do you think I'm that deranged? Do you!?" She screamed this second sentence, the flame from the fire flickering in her wide, dilated pupils. "Of course I experimented with dogs and cats, but they weren't enough."

Danny looked away, not wanting to give her the satisfaction that he believed her explanations were rational.

"It needs more than simple pets can offer. And I don't mean just their size."

Danny had no idea what the woman was implying with this last part.

"And after it fed on the first...person, it only wanted them from that point on. But I've used vagrants mostly. Older people and the homeless."

"And that somehow makes it better?"

"I'm sure it would have made it better had I used them this time!" the woman was in Danny's face now, screaming. "Instead of your wife! Or you!" She lowered her voice again. "It would have been someone nobody would have missed."

Danny suddenly thought about not being missed, and he wondered how long it would be until someone noticed that he and Tammy were gone. They had no family nearby, and the few members they had at all they spoke with maybe once or twice a month. And as far as friends were concerned, the truth was they had no real friends to speak of, and certainly none locally. The few they'd left when he and Tammy moved had families and obligations of their own. There might be one or two unreturned phone calls or emails, but that wouldn't raise any real suspicion. And since he and Tammy had no real jobs, there wouldn't be any employer to inquire about them when they didn't show up for work. Damn, Danny thought, his life was actually kind of sad.

"But it's been done for this cycle. It won't be coming back for more than a year."

"Why? Why only...one?"

"I've never known that part exactly. For years I would offer more men, one after the other, night after night, but it never mattered. It never came back until the next cycle. Even now, sporadically, I'll lure someone to the beach after six months or so, just to see..." Lynn frowned a genuine one of sadness, despair almost. "But it's always..."

"Fourteen months."

The woman smiled sadly now, calming herself, sitting back against the far wall of the cave across from Danny. "Exactly, fourteen months. Which means, unfortunately for you, I've no real reason to keep you alive? I'd like to, of course, seeing as you were the intended all along. But I couldn't sustain you for that long. Until the next time."

The woman took a deep breath and stood, looking around the cave as if with fresh, clear eyes, a satisfied smirk on her lips.

"But thank you for listening. It's been very cathartic to finally talk about it. You can't imagine the difficulty that comes with keeping this kind of secret. I've had no one to talk to about all of this for so many years."

"Not even to Tracy?"

"What?"

"Tracy. I believe she said you were her aunt. She told me you talked about these things all the time when she was younger."

How do you...When..?"

"She told me all about you, Lynn Shields, about the stories you used to tell her. Scary monster stories about sea creatures and such."

"I didn't tell her...those were just stories...as far as she knew anyway. Stories kids like to hear. She knew those weren't to be taken seriously." The look on Lynn's face was drawn tight now, struggling to hold on to control.

"Did she think that what happened to Lyle was to be taken seriously?" Danny asked. He had nothing to lose now, so he was going to play this hand to its end, laying all of his cards down on the table.

"What did you say?" Lynn Shields approached Danny, lifting the scythe as she did, shining the beam of the flashlight into his face.

"Lyle Bradford. I know all about him too. Does the name Sarah Needler ring a bell?"

Chapter 12

THE STORY HIT THE ROVE Beach Rover on Saturday morning, just over a week after Sarah's initial meeting with Danny Lynch. She'd not gotten him to tell his full story that afternoon in the bar, but something about her had made him trust her enough to send the pictures that now lay scattered about her desk.

The story had barely made the A section, one page from the back, and had been pared from 1,200 words to about 250, with several editorial additions that made the story sound like some kind of hoax, an April Fool's Day joke to be laughed at. Strap had included the photo, but it was especially grainy looking on the black-and-white paper, and the size was reduced to that of a thumbnail, so small it was almost useless as an addendum.

And there had been no mention of Lyle Bradford, despite Sarah detailing the facts of his drowning and the events that followed it—including the peculiar acts of his girlfriend on the beach the next day. She knew it was a long shot for the piece to make it into the paper at all, let alone with an implied accusation about a citizen of Rove Beach, one who also happened to still be living there. But Lynn Shields' role was crucial to make the piece work, despite the tabloid nature of the story and the Loch-Ness-Monster-style photograph,

Sarah tossed the paper on her dining room table and picked up the phone to call Tom Strap, but then placed it back in its cradle, knowing her protests would only be met with retorts about libel and lawsuits, and how she should be happy the story was there at all. *Besides,* he would say, *it's already printed. There's nothing I can do about it now.* And if she kept badgering, he would remind her that all she'd offered him as proof was the undeterminable shape in the photo; she had not a single quote from the source who had supposedly seen the thing up close.

Danny.

He had fallen off the face of the Earth. She'd called him relentlessly for two days after the photos arrived, left at least a dozen messages on his voice mail, and drove by his home on three separate occasions. She'd knocked on his door, but despite the car in the driveway (and likely one in the garage), there was no answer.

It was possible that he'd taken a vacation—and since she and Danny were hardly friends, he was under no obligation to keep her abreast of his travels—but this didn't sound right. He wouldn't have sent her those pictures and then disappeared. At least not willingly.

Sarah was going to give him one more day. If he didn't surface by this evening, she was going to start following some leads.

Chapter 13

LYNN SHIELDS ALMOST vomited at the picture on page A-8 of the Rove Beach Rover. It was her God, captured on camera and published for the world to see. It was only the top of him, barely capturing the bulky rise of his shoulders, but she would have recognized it even without the caption and three-paragraph story that followed. It was a story that, if it caught the attention of any publication outside of her own sleepy town, could end up drawing monster hunters from all over the world.

"Is There Something Lurking in the Waters Off Rove Beach?"

Does Rove Beach have its own version of the Loch Ness Monster, living just off the coast near mile marker 3?

A local resident recently reported a sighting that he claims is of a creature unknown to the modern world. Daniel Lynch witnessed and photographed the creature as it was submerging into the Atlantic the Thursday before last. He claims...

Lynn didn't finish the article, and instead, with a mind of ire and fury, began constructing plans about how she would stage her niece for next year's feeding.

Tracy.

The thought of her niece flipping off to some stranger about who her aunt was and the stories she used to tell was almost too much for her mind to process. Why did the subject even come up in the first place? Did Tracy know about the God as well? Was that the impetus behind her constant calls, asking if she could use the house for the weekend?

Or did the runner tell her?

Lynn hadn't known the name of the man in her grotto—she hadn't cared, frankly—but now she had no doubts that it was the 'Daniel Lynch' from the article. He'd known about it all along. He knew of her God prior to the other morning. Prior to his wife's killing. For how long exactly, she couldn't be sure, but, despite the weakness of his photograph—which she knew would be scoffed at by the vast majority of people who read the article—he had seen it with his own eyes. It was the reason he hadn't come to the beach alone, and instead brought his wife. He meant to show it off.

Or perhaps he'd even intended her as a sacrifice, just as Lynn had done with her lover a decade ago.

There wasn't any real evidence to support this second theory, and based on his reaction at the sight of her dismemberment, as well as her earlier conversation with the man, she quite doubted it. But it was possible. He had obviously been deliberate about keeping his knowledge of the creature a secret from her, and, if he had offered his wife to the beast, his reaction could still have been genuine. She had felt the same pain watching Lyle being torn apart ten years ago.

Her concern now, though, was Tracy. That her niece had even casually mentioned Lynn's God, and as lately as only a few days ago, was enough to raise Lynn's suspicions about what the girl knew. Add in the fact that the mention was to the man whose photo had just appeared in the local paper, well, that was simply too coincidental.

Lynn was slightly paranoid, she recognized that in her thinking, but the plan brewing in her mind would be carried out nevertheless. She would invite her niece—and Mark, of course—for a little summer festival next year, consummated, perhaps, with a sunrise picnic, just before the equinox, which was roughly when her calculations predicted the God would return. If possible, and if all the plans fell in just the right way, she could hone the plan to allow an offering of them both to the creature. She'd never seen it take more than one at a time—and even with this last feeding, it seemed disinterested in pursuing the runner—but she could up the stakes with Tracy and Mark and see if it could be done.

But her niece would be the main target. Her punishment would be served.

A thought swiftly planted in Lynn's head. *Had she ever used a woman before? Other than the wife of the runner, who was not the original offering but was taken as a result of wrong place and wrong time?* After a few moments of pondering this question, she knew the answer was 'No,' she'd never offered a woman, a statistic that was due mainly to the fact that the vast majority of homeless people were men, and that there was always the vague implication sex was a possibility for them. But only if they could find their way to the beach some time before dawn on a particular morning of Lynn's choosing.

The Beach. Her beautiful beach. What if the publication of the story made her beach no longer viable? What if this tiny article by that cunt of a reporter whom she hadn't thought about in ten years destroyed her paradise? This is the feeling of loss beach town residents must have been experiencing for decades, Lynn thought, once greedy developers got that twinkle in their eyes and then bulldozed into their quiet enclaves, constructing massive hotels and condos along the shore lines, flooding their once-quaint towns with condescending magpies and drunken sorority girls.

Would this be the fate of Rove Beach as well? It was already trending there. The runner and his wife were new to town, and there were a dozen other couples just like them that moved in every month.

Maybe she could leave? Was that possible? After all, it was the sounds of the minke that lured her God to the shores, not the beach itself. Though could she even know that for sure? Perhaps it was both, a perfect, unique combination of sound and something else—the water temperature or latitude of the town, perhaps—that brought it marching out of the sea to the dark shores every fourteen months.

And where would she go anyway? If she were to sell her home and leave, she'd never profit enough from the sale to be able to afford another home that was in such a secluded place directly on the ocean.

Lynn composed herself and thought about her prisoner now, whom she'd planned to dispose of tomorrow night, when the weather was forecast to turn and there would be little chance that any late night beach walkers would decide to go sauntering down her stretch of sand. It was a shame, she knew, to have to give up such a prime source of food as the runner—Daniel Lynch—especially since he was so aptly restrained in her grotto.

The grotto.

She'd had it built illegally by contractors—illegal themselves—back at the turn of the millennium, forging paperwork that "proved" she was lawyer, and threatening to pull all the necessary levers of litigation to have them deported if they didn't build the in-ground space to her precise specifications. She'd paid them, of course, but not much, and after two months of backbreaking work, the result was a relatively hidden cut-out in the side of one of the dunes that buffered against her backyard, complete with a thick piece of wood, acting as the door, which had been carved into the shape of an arch and wedged into the grotto opening.

Immediately following its completion, Lynn had planted dozens of tufts of wild beach grass around the door for camouflage, and then had bought a NO TRESPASSING sign at a Home Depot, erecting it directly in front of the grotto's entrance. And there it stood today, never tampered with or questioned. The dunes weren't her property, of course, which is why the grotto had to be dug mostly by hand and at odd hours, but the sign didn't make that claim; it simply kept people away. And despite the crowds of locals that frequented her stretch of beach in season, it drew little attention from city officials.

When she'd first come up with the idea of a seaside prison, the year after her first feeding, it had seemed an absolute necessity. How else was she going to keep her victims contained and silent—and alive—until the God finally arrived? At that time, she'd no real formula or estimation regarding its arrival, so she figured she could keep a prisoner, bound, pulse barely detectable, and then drag the person night after night to the beach, where she would wait for the feeding.

But the work of keeping a person captive was far more gruelling than she'd ever anticipated. In addition to the responsibilities of feeding, watering and warmth, Lynn seemed to spend every moment away from the grotto on edge, distracted and irritable, or laying sleepless in her bed, wondering if the prisoner had removed its hand ties and gag and was now on the brink of escape. And the constant back-and-forth from the grotto to her home was more than mildly suspicious, an invitation for some Nosey Rosie to 'have concerns' and call the police.

So the grotto had sat empty almost every year since its construction. Lynn still made a point to check on it occasionally, but that was only to ensure it was still structurally viable. And those maintenance checks had paid off. Here she was now using it, and for just the incarceratory purposes for which it was designed.

Lynn stepped out to her lanai and looked down at the top of the dunes below, knowing that Daniel Lynch was beneath them, gagged and bound and likely sleeping. She stared up at the sky and the storm clouds that were approaching. At dark the rain would begin to fall.

She followed the path down to the beach and walked a hundred yards or so past the hidden grotto to where a tarp-covered object sat buttressed against the dunes. She grabbed the tarp at the front and pulled it up and backward, revealing a small, two-person ocean kayak, a leftover from the days of her cohabitation with Lyle. It was something they had bought together, just days before their short-lived engagement.

Lynn gripped the inside hull of the kayak on either side and walked backwards with it, slowly dragging the boat across the heavy sand, digging her heels deep, her thighs burning all the way until the kayak laid positioned next to the NO TRESPASSING sign, just outside the grotto entrance. It would be difficult work to get the runner in the boat and the boat on the water, but she'd accomplished more difficult tasks before. In any case, he would have to be sent to sea, and so as not to risk him floating up to the shore in front of her house a few days later, she would take him out as far as necessary.

Chapter 14

DANNY AWOKE TO THE sound of rustling outside the cave. He smelled piss, and felt the warmth of his own urine between his legs and down the back of his left thigh. The vague glow of moonlight filled the short space of the runway that led away from his prison, and then it was abruptly replaced by the beam of a flashlight. He could hear the steady downfall of rain.

Danny squinted at the bobbing ray approaching him, his sun-deprived eyes trying desperately to adjust.

"I always intended to install a toilet in here," the woman said. "Just a dirt hole really, nothing involving plumbing or pipes, of course." Danny could see Lynn Shields' crouching knees below the light beam. "But it was just one of those things that I never got to. You have things like that, I'm sure. Is that so, Daniel Lynch?"

Danny's nearly-closed eyes clicked halfway open at the sound of his name, and an abstract hope welled inside him, though he couldn't have said why.

"Anyway, it seems you don't need one anymore." Then, sounding to Danny almost as if it was an afterthought, Lynn Shields said, "And it's not going to matter in few hours." The woman paused a moment and looked up and to her left, searching the possibilities in her mind. "But perhaps I'll still have it done." She nodded, as if the decision had been made.

Danny wanted to speak, but his throat and lips felt like sandpaper.

"I have a question for you though, before we begin with what comes next. You never told me that you had seen it before. Before the other night when your wife...you did tell me she was your wife, correct?" The woman paused, allowing Danny the opportunity to confirm or correct the relationship.

Danny nodded.

"But then this very morning, a picture appeared in the papers with your name written right next to it."

"Sarah." The name barely passed over Danny's lips.

"Yes. Sarah Needler. So though you were a little deceitful about what all you knew regarding the Ocean God, it seems you *were* telling the truth about the reporter. And her suspicions about me. But what of this picture, Daniel? You never mentioned any picture. Are there other secrets you've been keeping from me?"

"Danny."

"Of course. Danny. What else have you seen, Danny?" The woman's expression fell flat, abandoning any playfulness that may have existed in her demeanor.

Danny peeled his lips apart as if to speak, but instead let his tongue fall out, just over his bottom lip, the tip barely outside the boundary of his mouth. He was starving for water, and this seemed like a universal symbol to express that.

Lynn smiled and rolled her eyes, as if humored by her forgetfulness, like she'd forgotten to ask Danny how his summer vacation had gone. She brought a full bottle of water from her bag, and Danny could see the cloudy liquid inside, indicating it was cold. He closed his eyes and dipped his head back in ecstasy at the thought of it.

"Just a few drops so you can get that voice working, huh? And then, depending on what I hear from you, you can have more. Does that sound fair?"

Danny nodded. He would have agreed to anything.

Lynn twisted the cap and tipped the bottle against Danny's lips, once again hydrating her prisoner into obedience. She allowed him a few seconds to let the moisture do its work, and then she nodded at him to begin, sitting down in front of him like a kindergartner at story time.

Danny swallowed and licked his lips. "I saw it last Thursday," he began. "I guess you probably know this, but I'm at the beach around the same time every morning six days a week. At least I used to be."

Danny tossed out the subtle bluff by accident, but hearing it spoken seemed to imply that he would be missed if he didn't keep his regular schedule. Of course, there was no real logic in that hope, considering that he always came to the beach alone and his wife, the woman already knew, was dead. Lynn Shields just stared expressionless at Danny.

"I swam in the ocean for a few minutes, like always, and then..."

"Then what?"

"I saw you. You know that. You saw me see you."

"Yes, yes! I know about all of that! After! After that!" Danny knew the irritation in the woman's voice was not due to any redundancy, but rather was a mask to cover her lament at having missed seeing it that morning, knowing she was so close.

"I was on my way to leave when I heard a loud, thumping splash, and then I turned to see...the thing I saw."

"Not the thing," the woman said calmly, with quiet instruction. "The God." She waited a beat, as if to make sure Danny had received this titular lesson, and then said, "And what did he do?" Her eyes were wide with anticipation, and, reflexively, she scooted forward a few inches.

"He walked out of the ocean."

"How? Explain it!"

"It was a slow, I don't know, methodical walk, like it...the God...had a purpose. And then he just stood there. Staring. Looking up toward *your* house, actually. I don't know, it was like he was looking for you. Expecting you. Like you talked about earlier."

Tears had begun to roll steadily from the woman's eyes, and she took a deep breath and swallowed. "Yes," she said, nodding in understanding. "And what else? Please, continue."

Danny felt drained from the story; his mouth was parched and the lack of food had made him sleepy again. "Not much," he said, closing his eyes. "He turned and walked back to the sea. I was able to take a few pictures." Danny licked his lips with a tongue that was once again dry and desperate. "And now here we are."

"Yes, we are," Lynn said, wiping the tears from her eyes. She stood tall, and Danny could feel the woman studying him before she walked back to the opening of the prison dune, pushing the leaning door away and stepping out to the beach. Danny could see her feet in the flashlight beam, and the rain splashing down around them.

She was gone for less than five minutes, and when she returned, crouching again toward him down hall of the burrow, Danny could see she was holding a gun in her hand.

Chapter 15

LYNN WASN'T ENTIRELY sure that her plan would work—that Danny Lynch would follow her instructions—but she felt she had him hungry and thirsty enough that his delirium would make him more obedient than he normally would be in his situation. A sort of Stockholm syndrome, she thought, though that didn't sound quite right.

She had considered killing him in the cave, at which point she would somehow drag him to the boat and slowly load him in before shoving them both out to sea. But the physical effort required to carry out that plan was likely beyond her, as the runner was no less than a hundred and seventy-five pounds and she no giant herself.

And the risk of being seen wasn't to be dismissed either. She'd never be able to explain away some witness's vision of her hauling a limp man's body across the empty beach. And when the runner ultimately was reported missing, which, at some point, despite his apparent lack of connections, he would be, the dots could easily be connected to her. It was one of the most wonderful things about the God and her sacrifices to him, she thought: there were no loose ends.

"Here is how things are going to happen," she started. "I'm going to cut one of your hands free, and then you're going to take the knife and cut the other one free. I'm going to be standing here, just as I am now, with this gun pointed at your belly. After you cut your second hand free, you're going to toss the knife to my feet. Then, when I tell you, you're going to get on your hands and knees in a crawling position. I would add 'slowly' to those last instructions, but I imagine your legs are fairly weak at this point, so I don't think that part will be an issue. Once you're on your knees, you're going to crawl toward the grotto entrance—the place where I've been entering and exiting. Are things clear so far?"

Danny was wide awake now and staring at the woman alertly. He was abstractly scared and angry, but his fear and anger were overwhelmed by hunger and dehydration.

He nodded.

"Once we're on the beach, there will be further instructions." She paused. "And at that point, you can have this."

Lynn Shields pulled a sandwich from her bag. It was thick and round and tightly wrapped in cellophane, and Danny could see the ham and lettuce and smudges of mayonnaise pressing up against the store-bought casing. He could feel his salivary glands trying to react, but the moisture simply wasn't there.

"Let's go."

Lynn cut the first rope free, and from that point, the rest of the plan went without incident. Within a few minutes, she and Danny Lynch were standing on the dark beach with a steady rain falling around them. The rainfall had increased slightly over the last few minutes, and it seemed intent on getting stronger as the morning approached.

Lynn stood about eight feet away from her prisoner, the gun pointed at his chest, watching him devour the convenience store sandwich like a circus geek who had just been tossed a fish head.

"We're going to take a trip, Danny."

Her prisoner glanced up for just a moment, his mouth full and eyes wild, and then returned his focus to the sandwich. He reminded Lynn of some predator on the savannah, teeth deep into a fresh kill, unable to be torn from its food except when its perimeter has been pressed too closely by some brave scavenger.

Danny swallowed the last of the sandwich in a giant gulp and then uttered, "Water."

Lynn had the flashlight in one hand and the pistol in the other. She had placed the two duffle bags, one of which contained the remaining water bottle, in the boat in preparation for their excursion. "Come on," she said, "it's in the boat. You take a couple of swigs, and then you're going to drag that thing down to the water." Lynn nodded once toward the vessel.

"And food. Is there any more food?"

"You keep cooperating like you're doing and we'll see."

Lynn waved the gun toward the boat and waited for Danny to pass her, and then followed behind him at an arm's reach. The runner seemed incapable even of thinking about dissent at this point, so focused was he still on his immediate physiological needs. But still, she needed to be careful.

"There, in that one on the left. There's water in that one. Be real slow though, Danny."

The rain was falling heavily now, and water was accumulating quickly in the hull of the boat. She'd made a mistake by removing the tarp beforehand, but she hadn't wanted to waste any more time than was necessary when this moment arrived. Now those meager saved seconds would be swallowed up and multiplied waiting for the boat to drain.

She watched Danny as he rummaged in the duffel bag, moving so slowly he seemed to be falling in and out of sleep. "What is taking so long?"

Danny stood up slowly with this back to Lynn, and then turned toward her, his movements zombielike. As he stood in the beam, Lynn could see that his motions matched his look, which appeared close to death. His eyes were barely open and he was wavering in the storm, the duffel bag hanging limply in his hand by his side. Had she really malnourished him that much that quickly? He seemed relatively well in the cave, considering, but perhaps the sudden requirement of effort had taken some grave toll on his body.

He opened his mouth now and let the rainwater fall haphazardly into his mouth. "Food?

"You said water. That bag in your hand has the water."

The runner looked down at his hand and stared at it, confused.

"Oh for Christ's sake, we don't have time for this."

Lynn waved the gun toward the other bag on the stern seat, and then she let her hand hang down in frustration past her hip so that the gun was vertical by her thigh. She took a step towards the boat and scoffed as she illuminated the duffel with the flashlight.

"It's there!" she screamed.

Lynn had formed an insult about her prisoner's intelligence in her brain, but before she could send the thought across her lips, she felt the smash of the water-bottle-filled duffel across her face.

DANNY WAS INDEED DESPERATE—HUNGRY and tired—and the sandwich tasted as remarkable as he had hoped. But the mannerisms he made while ravaging the meal were exaggerated, inspired by movies where the dead became alive and, for some unknown reason, decided to become cannibals. There was no real vision attached to his ravenous actions, at least in terms of an end goal, but he had to try something, vaguely hoping that his odd behavior would lead to some type of distraction. All he needed was a moment, one tiny window when the guard came down and he could take his shot, in whatever form that presented itself.

"We're going to take a trip Danny." Lynn said, her voice hinting at something not quite sympathetic, but not altogether evil either.

Danny assumed the 'trip' Lynn was planning was to be some type of short ocean voyage, launched from these shores in the boat that lie on the sand before him, and ending with his dead body being dumped overboard somewhere off the stormy coast of Rove Beach.

But he vowed not to leave the world like that.

If he was going to die tonight, it was going to be on the sand of this beach, his body pocked with bullet holes. What this crazy bitch did with his corpse afterward was out of his control. Whatever his fate was to be, though, Danny had no intentions of making it easy.

"Water," he said, straining his voice just enough to be heard above the rain.

"Come on, it's in the boat. You take a couple of swigs, and then you're going to drag that thing down to the water."

Danny was damn thirsty, but he knew this answer from Lynn Shields was the opportunity he was looking for, and even if it turned out to be unsuccessful, it was the only one he was likely to get.

"And food. Is there any more food?" Danny thought this additional request was a nice touch, if he did say so himself. He thought it made him sound delirious, broken.

"You keep cooperating like you're doing and we'll see."

He moved slowly to the boat, slower than he'd been moving at any time up to this point. His leg hurt and he was exhausted, but not quite to the extent he was showing. He reached the boat and stopped directly in front of it, maintaining his bewildered act throughout.

"There, in that one on the left. There's water in that one. Be real slow though, Danny."

Danny reached into the hull and felt the heft of the duffel immediately. He placed his hand inside the bag and then exhaled silently, closing his eyes and smiling as he wrapped his hand around the full bottle of water. The taut label and bulge of plastic at the neck and shoulders felt as divine as any woman's body he'd ever known.

The bottle had yet to be opened, and, of course, the fullness of it was key. Had even a little bit of water been drunk from it, the plastic of the bottle would give upon impact and the effectiveness of the blow would be diminished.

But this bottle was beautiful—factory-sealed and lethal.

"What is taking so long?"

This was the decisive moment. If Danny stood and turned too quickly, or even looked a touch too alert while holding the bag in his hand, the woman was likely to shoot him dead. Danny didn't know much about Lynn Shields, but he did know one thing undoubtedly: she would not hesitate to kill him.

He involuntarily summoned the feelings of a prisoner of war, or as close to that destitution as he could get without ever experiencing the horror himself. He turned to the woman and looked past her, as if so close to the end that he was unable even to focus on the imminent murderer before him. He let his lips open and his tongue fall out to taste the rain.

"Food?"

"You said water. That bag in your hand has the water."

Danny heard the frustration immediately. The fish was on the line, now it was time to reel her in. He looked down at his hand, morphing his face into one of pain and disorder.

"Oh for Christ's sake, we don't have time for this."

And there it was. She'd lost control, just as he suspected she would, and as Danny watched the hand holding the gun drop to the woman's hip, he gripped the neck of the duffel with all the might to which his fingers would consent. He held the bag like a hammer, the head of which was a 16.9 ounce bottle of Dasani.

The woman took a step toward him, and Danny swung like Thor.

Chapter 16

"HI, MY NAME IS SARAH Needler. I'm looking for your aunt."

Tracy Amato squinted at the woman who was standing outside her door, a look of confusion and irritation draped across her face. "What...what time is it?"

It was just past 6:30 in the morning and it was raining like hell. "It's almost 7."

It hadn't taken long for Sarah to track down Lynn Shields' niece; she was well known in Rove Beach, as well as in her adjacent hometown of Portsmouth. But Sarah had told herself one more day, that was it, and then she'd start looking for Danny.

"Did you try her house?" Tracy asked.

"There was no answer." Sarah hadn't tried approaching Lynn Shields, having experienced the pointlessness of that during her interview ten years ago. She thought of driving by her residence, perhaps doing a quick walk around the oceanside house to scope it out, but after finding out that her niece was a frequent guest there, Sarah decided the inroad through her would be a bit less rocky.

Tracy continued her bewildered stare at Sarah, still groggy with sleep, and then a glean of recognition appeared in her eyes. She scoffed and shook her head slowly. "This is about that picture in yesterday's paper, isn't it? I can't believe it. Mark was right. He told me this was going to happen. This is just great."

"It...kind of is about that, yes." Lynn replied, slightly impressed with the girl's instincts. "Why would you assume that?"

"I don't know. Maybe because in twenty three years no one has ever come to my door—certainly not before sunrise—asking about Aunt Lynn. And now today, the day after some weird sea monster pops up in the paper, here *you* are."

"But what does she have to do with the picture in the paper?" Sarah, of course, suspected quite a bit about what Lynn Shields' had to do with it—after all, she was at her niece's door asking questions—but years of experience had taught Sarah that when you had a talker on the line, you let 'em talk. "Has she seen it too?"

"I don't know about that, but I heard way too many stories growing up to know that if anyone in this state knows about a sea monster off the Carolina coast, it's Lynn Shields. She has, like, a cult thing about stuff like that."

"Stuff like that?"

"Mythical creatures, I guess you would call them. Bigfoot and pygmies and things of that nature."

Sarah considered informing Tracy that pygmies were, in fact, real, but she let it go. "Really?"

"She's crazy, I'm telling you."

Sarah nodded politely, trying to keep the urgency she felt inside from surfacing. She'd been up most of the night with worry, and as the morning approached, she now truly suspected Danny was in peril. Perhaps even dead.

But she also knew that girls like Tracy sometimes got spooked when pushed too hard. *Just ease her in,* she thought. *Don't get too Jane Detective on her.* "Cool. Well, listen Tracy, I'm doing a follow-up story on the sighting and—"

"You're a reporter?"

Sarah smirked and shrugged, and then shook her head with a dismissive shiver, as if 'reporter' were too lofty a title for what she did. "A freelancer. Just a hobby really."

Tracy studied Sarah for a few beats and then nodded approvingly. "Cool. I mean I don't know much, just stuff Aunt Lynn told me over the years. What do you want to hear?"

"I'd love to hear some of the stories she told you as a kid. You know, as long as you weren't sworn to secrecy or anything."

Tracy shrugged and shook her head. "I don't care. They're just stories; there were never any secrets behind them as far as I know. And most of them are kind of silly."

Tracy's stories were actually quite riveting, and the young woman was a far more compelling storyteller than Sarah would ever have suspected. Sarah considered this was because she, Sarah, now had to consider the truth of at least one of them.

The first few Tracy told were to do with witches and spells, fantasy stories about mastery of the elements and that type of thing. But it was the story of the Ocean God that got Sarah's attention. This is the one that matched up quite well with the story of Danny's sighting.

"'He comes every year plus two,' she would tell us, meaning fourteen months, 'marching from the depths of the sea toward his sand-bound victim, who lay helpless and ignorant, placed there by his master of the shore.'" Sarah snickered. "She would tell it just like that, real old-timey and mysterious, like she was sitting around a bubbling cauldron with steam rising up around her."

Tracy laughed aloud now at this descriptive notion, not seeming to consider that the story she was recounting contained a character very similar to the one in the picture on her kitchenette table.

"'Lured by the cries of the minke'" Tracy continued, "'It is drawn at dawn each day for not more than two weeks, taking one victim and one alone. Once sated for the season, it returns to the Atlantic, where it begins its wait again.'"

Sarah felt the bulge in her throat and a chill spill down her back, one which expanded out to the rest of her body, nearly freezing her with terror. "At dawn?"

Tracy shrugged. "That's how the story went. Are you okay, Ms. Needler?"

Sarah checked her watch. It was five minutes after seven. "What time is sunrise?" she asked rhetorically, and with far more frenzy than she'd intended.

"I don't know. It's still pretty dark out because of the rain, but probably soon. But...wait, do you believe in this? You think the Ocean God story is about that thing in the paper?"

Sarah was on her feet now, gathering her notes and shoving them into her bag. "Thank you, Tracy, you've been a big help."

"Where are you going?"

"Um...I have to get back to the office. I have a deadline to meet for this story."

"What 'office?' I thought you said you were a freelancer."

"They...uh...sometimes let me use their office for writing." Sarah was at the door now. She turned to Tracy and extended her hand. "Thank you again, Tracy."

Tracy calmed her expression now and looked at Sarah sternly. "Is this a real thing? Because if it is, I want to see it."

Sarah held her stare for a moment and then walked out the door, Tracy following behind her.

Chapter 17

THE BOTTLE LANDED SQUARELY on Lynn Shields' jaw, and the resistance in Danny's hand was ecstasy. He absently wondered if that was the first time in his life he'd ever struck another human with all his force, and then decided it was.

The sound of distress that erupted from the woman's mouth was a mixture of startle and pain, and the result of the blow opened the only window Danny was going to get. If he missed this opportunity, he was dead; there was no room for hesitation.

Through the beam of the tumbling flashlight and the dim glow of the nearly-risen sun, Danny watched Lynn stumble backwards from the boat and then instinctively run several more yards in retreat, creating as much distance as possible between her and her assaulter. Dawn had almost reached the beach, and he could see that she hadn't entirely lost her balance and was still on her feet, facing backwards, less than ten yards away from him.

Danny also noted that the gun hadn't discharged, which suggested she had dropped it along with the flashlight. But it was still a guess, and since he couldn't see the firearm in either her hand or the sand, he had to assume she still had it. His instinct was to continue attacking the woman with his water-filled sack, to beat her with it until she was bloody and unconscious. But he couldn't take the chance if she still had the weapon. All he could do now was run.

Danny's legs were weakened from lack of use during his short time in captivity, and the heavy wet sand made running a nightmare. But he gave his full effort, relentlessly fighting the burn in his thighs and hips, and as he slowly progressed past the boat, trudging south toward the pier, he coughed out a tiny laugh, knowing that just a few more yards and he'd be at the next beach access and only a few seconds from escape.

And then came the shots.

One, two, three, four, five. They came in such rapid succession that Danny never knew which one of the bullets hit him, but the force on his upper back and right shoulder felt as if he'd been blindsided by a wrecking ball.

He fell to the sand instantly, as if he'd tripped over a hidden wire that had been extended from the dunes to the water. His left cheek was buried in the sand, arms in arrest position beside him, and Danny watched in horror as cloudy red rivulets of water flowed chaotically past his eyes, desperately making their way from his shoulder to the sea.

He tried to rise again, but the instant he lifted his torso, two more rounds whizzed above him, collapsing him back to his stomach. The impact on his injured shoulder sent sheets of cold pain through his body, and for the first time in Danny's life, he said a prayer of death.

SHE'D PUT SEVEN ROUNDS in the gun, a move she thought of as especially prudent at the time, never imagining she'd need to fire even one. But now the last had been fired and the gun was empty.

Lynn was irritated with her last reaction—there was no reason to fire those final two shots, especially from that distance and with as little visibility as she had in the storm—but she could see the runner attempting to get to his feet and she panicked.

It didn't matter though. She knew that he'd been hit with at least one of the shots and was now hurt. Hurt and emotionally beaten. And there would be no dropping of her guard this time; she'd been fooled once and thus not again.

Lynn looked west toward the sky in the distance and saw nothing but blackness. The clouds hung like soiled drapes, indicating the storm was likely to last for several more hours. It was a blessing, of course, since the heavy rain would keep any beachgoers and deck viewers away for the bulk of the morning. But all it took was one set of eyeballs; she needed to get her prisoner off the beach soon.

A giant crash of thunder exploded to the east, startling her to its attention. Lynn pivoted and looked to the ocean. She stood staring in awe as she watched the waves, enthralled by their battle with each other and the ferocity with which they jockeyed for position as they fought toward the shoreline. Even if everything had gone as planned, she thought, without the attempted escape of Danny Lynch, there would have been no way to get the boat anywhere close to the distance necessary to dump his body in a place where it would disappear forever. It was foolish for her to have even devised it, considering the forecast.

But none of it mattered now. With one swing of a satchel, her plan had collapsed, and her only current option was to bring the runner back to the grotto. There she would have to accomplish things in a more traditional way. His corpse would deteriorate quickly in the cave, and the smell, she knew, was likely to become an issue, possibly exposing the existence of her dirt dungeon once the weather cleared and people returned to the beach. But she wouldn't allow him to sit more than a day or two. The next calm day would see her out on the water hours before dawn, the body of Danny Lynch in tow.

Lynn walked toward the man lying on his stomach, fighting against the wind and rain as she approached, and then stood over him with the gun—empty and impotent—pointed at the back of his head. "Turn over," she said, speaking as loudly as she could above the sound of the storm.

No movement.

"Turn over!" she repeated. She was screaming now, her body leaning forward with her shoulders back, neck craned.

Slowly, the runner extended his left arm into the sand, straight above his head, and then rolled over onto his left side. His right arm followed reluctantly, flopping limply to the sand and producing a tortured scream from the man.

"Now stand up."

Danny Lynch took a deep breath and then grimaced as he sat up, hanging his head between his knees before finally rising to his feet. His head was bowed as he stood there, his eyes on the ground at his feet, but as he looked up and faced Lynn, she thought she detected a flicker of terror in them, just a flash really, instantaneous in its length, some look of dread that went beyond the certainty of his own, momentary death. It was the delirium again, she figured. She would think of that look only once again, and the thought would last for only a fraction of a second, just before the last air of life left her body.

Danny moved to his left, sideways, almost stumbling, and then he stopped so that his back was to the dunes and he was facing the ocean. Lynn moved the quarter circle with him, squaring him off, remaining face-to-face with her hostage, her back now to the ocean.

"That's it," she said. "I can't blame you for that attempt; though, of course, you will have to pay for it."

"I thought we were going for an outing." Danny grunted, holding his left elbow with his good hand, pinning the wounded arm against his body.

Lynn recognized that if she didn't get the man off the beach in the next minute or two, he was going to collapse from blood loss, and at that point she would be forced to drag him. "We're going to head back to the grotto, Danny. It seems this wasn't the best day for a boat ride after all. Let's go." She waved the gun in the direction of the dune cave.

"I need a doctor."

"You'll need a medical examiner." Lynn snapped out her reply almost before Danny had finished his sentence. She could feel that her eyes were wide now, crazed, and she was no longer interested in her own restraint. She just needed to get him back in the grotto, that was priority one; once he was back in control, she would head up to the house to find another bullet. The death shot had to come now, this morning, while the storm was still raging and the report would be muffled by the cacophony of the storm.

"I want to see it with you. I can help you."

Lynn wasn't entirely sure she had heard the words correctly—the man was barely audible in the wind—but she responded as if she had.

"You can help me with what, Danny?"

The runner stared at her, his eyes half-open, his jaw clenched as if anticipating a shot from a needle. The dripping rain from his hair and face made him look like a madman. "You know."

Lynn swallowed and stared back. She *had* heard him correctly, and her eyes were now fixed on him, eager. She imagined she must have looked like a child on Christmas morning. Finally, she broke herself from the spell of possibility, the thoughts of having a partner in the miracle of the God. She'd considered it once before, with her lover and once future husband, but that had ended like all the rest of them.

Lynn replaced her somber, hopeful look with a wide smile. "You can't help me, Daniel Lynch. It's over. Your words are those of desperation. What wouldn't you say to convince me to let you go?"

Danny stayed silent.

"I know you believe me to be crazy. And I understand that thinking. The fact is, I am a bit crazy. I've lived alone for so many years now that I must be. But I'm also right. You saw it yourself."

"I did see it, Lynn, that's why I want to help you."

Lynn studied the man's face, his eyes were wide, and his breathing was heavy and labored.

"It was amazing. The most amazing thing I've ever seen."

"Yes," Lynn whispered.

"And I want to see it again. And you're the only one that knows how to summon it."

The runner stood like a statue in front of her, the sheets of rain so thick around him that his very presence had become a blur.

"It would have been possible once, Danny. But it's too late for you now. It's too late fo—"

"No Lynn. It's too late for you."

The first thing she felt was the warmth on the side of her head, followed by darkness as the long, crusty fingers wrapped around her eyes and forehead. She tried to run, to break the grip, but she was immediately pulled backwards, her feet now dangling above the sand. "No!" she screamed instinctively, and then followed it with a more tempered, "How?"

The God spread his fingers slightly, to get a better grip on her skull, Lynn presumed, and she could see the runner standing unmoved from his position. His eyes were fixed on the event happening in front of him, and Lynn knew instantly the feeling he was experiencing.

He was drifting farther away with every second, and Lynn felt the pressure at her temples as she was being dragged down toward the water. *How can it be back?* she wondered.

But the answer came almost instantaneously. *It was supposed to be him. But it took the woman instead.*

The first woman.

"Women!" she screamed into the dawn air, feeling some primal obligation to reveal this secret before she died.

Lynn Shields had one more revelation—that the look she had detected in the runner's eyes just moments ago wasn't delirium at all; it was from the monster approaching her from behind.

It was her last thought before her skull and brain were crushed by the force of her own God.

Chapter 18

DESPITE THE THUNDER, Danny recognized the crash in the ocean instantly. It was the same one he'd heard several mornings ago, during a time when his life was still one of idleness and routine. The weather that day had been tranquil, and there had been no thunder for the sound to compete with, but Danny knew it was the same sound. He'd never forget it.

"Turn over." The voice was a whisper in Danny's ears, and he first thought it may be the wind. "Turn over!"

Danny obeyed the command this time, managing to fight through the pain in his arm and the dizziness in his head to get his back to the sand and then forward to his seat. With what he imagined was nearly the last of his energy, he rose to his feet. Any more effort beyond that was going to take a miracle.

And then he saw it, and the miracle he needed was suddenly produced in his body in the form of adrenaline.

Rising from the ocean like an ancient deity, something devised in the mythology of the Greeks perhaps, or maybe something more eastern—Japanese or Indian—was the mysterious animal of the sea, the one that had changed the course of his life in mere seconds.

Danny felt his eyes flicker, but there was little more that escaped him in terms of a notable reaction. Had he been fully coherent, healthy and properly nourished, he never could have maintained the subtlety of his response to the approaching beast. But as things were at that point, so close to death anyway, Danny managed to allow only the smallest trace of fear to show.

The massive creature was approaching Lynn from her back, but also slightly to her side on the left. Even if he could stall the woman long enough for the thing to reach her, she would eventually see it coming from the angle at which she was currently standing. To mitigate this possibility, Danny took a few steps to his left, and, thankfully, Lynn mimed him, thus maintaining the proper coordinates. She now had her back directly toward the creature.

"That's it," she said. "I can't blame you for that attempt; though, of course, you will have to pay for it."

Danny wasn't sure what better 'payment' he could give than his very life, which this lunatic was clearly planning on taking, leaving his body to be torn apart by lemon sharks somewhere off the coast of Rove Beach. But his goal now wasn't to debate semantics; what Danny needed to do now was keep her on the beach. For just another minute or two.

"I thought we were going for an outing," he said, the words coming out garbled and weak. Danny assumed this was a result of his light-headedness, which itself was a result of the blood he was losing from his shoulder at a frightening rate. Perhaps the thing approaching wasn't real after all and was just a hallucination. Danny felt a twinge of sadness at this thought, praying it wasn't the case.

"We're going to head back to the grotto, Danny. It seems this wasn't the best day for a boat ride after all. Let's go."

Danny ignored her wave of the gun and stood his ground. "I need a doctor."

"You'll need a medical examiner."

Danny could hear that whatever sanity was left in the woman was quickly draining. If he continued stonewalling, passively resisting her commands, he'd be shot where he stood. Lynn Shields had certainly done crazier things in her life than shoot a man in cold blood. In fact, according to her, she murdered someone at a rate of almost one per year for the last twenty years or so.

"I want to see it with you," he pled. Danny narrowed his eyes and swallowed, trying to elicit an expression of sympathy and understanding toward the woman, an effort to communicate that he could understand the ecstasy of the thing she cherished most in the world.

The giant creature was so close now, and Danny closed his eyes for a beat and then opened them slowly, again testing if he was indeed experiencing reality. The thing remained in Danny's line of sight, the howl of the wind keeping it as silent as a butterfly as it approached.

Danny narrowed his eyes further until they were mere slits, using all of his will to keep focused on Lynn and not the creature pressing forward. He knew that if he looked over her shoulder, directly at the 'God,' he would reveal its presence to her. Slouching toward her.

Danny's mind drifted to the poem by Yeats. He was pretty sure the title was "The Second Coming." *Those were some groovy lyrics*, he thought, and then wondered if he'd just spoken that thought aloud.

No! Another minute! He forced his mind back, trying desperately to stay conscious and in the moment. "I can help you," he said.

The woman hesitated, and Danny wondered if she had heard him, or, again, whether the words had actually crossed his lips at all.

"You can help me with what, Danny?"

She had heard him all right, and the creature was only steps away now.

The size of the monster was dizzying, and Danny now doubted the chances of his survival. He would collapse soon, and even if the creature took Lynn first, it would certainly come back for him, especially as he would be unconscious in less than a minute or two. Clearly Lynn had been wrong about it taking only one person per cycle—after all, here it was again—so it was almost a certainty that Danny wouldn't be leaving the beach alive either.

"You know," he managed.

Lynn swallowed and stared back at him, her eyes now fixed with an expression indicating she may be open to his offer. But the look lasted only a moment. She smiled at him now, as if tickled that Danny would have had the audacity to try yet another trick.

"You can't help me, Daniel Lynch. It's over. Your words are those of desperation. What wouldn't you say to convince me to let you go?"

Danny said nothing, knowing that pleading against this particular point would only reinforce it.

"I know you believe me to be crazy. And I understand that thinking. The fact is, I am a bit crazy. I've lived alone for so many years now that I must be. But I'm also right. You saw it yourself."

The creature was now standing directly behind the woman, towering above her like a tree. Its eyes were narrow, slanted in an expression of pain and struggle. The rain was bouncing off its smooth black head, and its mouth was moving up and down in a slow chomping motion, steady and wide, as if stretching its jaws for the impending meal.

Danny never let his eyes waver to it completely. "I did see it, Lynn," he slurred, "that's why I want to help you." He paused. "It was amazing. The most amazing thing I've ever seen."

"Yes."

"And I want to see it again. And you're the only one that knows how to summon it." Danny stood motionless now. He'd done what he could do, almost impossibly keeping this act alive.

He watched the creature open its arms wide, stretching them completely out to either side of its body.

"It would have been possible once, Danny. But it's too late for you now. It's too late fo—"

Danny watched the gun fall from the woman's hand as the God grasped its prey. "No Lynn," he said, "it's too late for you."

The creature gripped his victim by the sides of her head, and Danny watched in wonder as its long fingers nearly enveloped Lynn Shields' face. It pulled her effortlessly away toward the water, and Danny had a sudden vision of his wife's death.

How I wish I could see that again, he thought, and then he blinked the idea away in shame.

"No! How?"

Lynn's eyes appeared for a moment between a gap in the thing's fingers, and Danny almost smiled at her expression of helplessness. He'd never felt anything close to what he was feeling. He couldn't take his eyes off the carnage.

The power of it. The purpose.

With every step the creature took, Lynn Shields was pulled farther from Danny's vision, so he took a step forward each time the creature stepped back, ensuring he kept the beautiful massacre within viewing distance. He wanted this sight—this feeling—to last forever.

Danny watched the struggle dwindle, with Lynn Shields' head narrowing as the bone that was her skull began to give. But she said one word before the final crush, before her eyes exploded from their sockets to the sand below.

"Women!" she shouted desperately. It was a haunting word, and one that would possess Danny from that point on.

Women. He had it figured within moments.

The creature had taken Danny's wife, and that's why it returned. That was the difference between this feeding and every one before it. Lynn Shields had always used men. Why else would she have screamed that word?

Danny formulated a few more thoughts in his mind, and began to approach what could perhaps become a working theory—one that could guide him going forward in his new life.

But before all of the pieces had locked into place, he collapsed to the ground, the wound in his shoulder leaking blood like a ruptured oil tanker as the rain fell all around him.

Chapter 19

SARAH SAW HIM FIRST from the landing and immediately called 911.

"Are we too late?" Tracy asked. "Is he dead?"

Sarah walked slowly down the steps, almost too afraid to find out the answer to Tracy's question.

"Was that the Ocean God that did this?"

Sarah hesitated. "Maybe, but I don't think so. I don't think he would be here at all if it was the..." She knew the sighting was real now, but wasn't quite ready to acknowledge it by name. "Whatever it is."

The two women reached the sand and then sprinted toward Danny's body. Sarah immediately placed her hand on his neck beneath the chin and took a huge sigh. "Get your shirt off," she ordered, removing her own jacket and pulling off her blouse. "He needs something dry to put around this wound."

The sirens were screaming in the distance.

"Who did this?" Tracy asked. "He's shot? What is going on?"

Sarah placed the two shirts on either side of Danny's body, the bullet having entered and exited at his shoulder. Sarah was no doctor, but she got the sense this was a good sign. She looked up at the young girl. "It's your aunt, Tracy. There's something you need to know about her."

Chapter 20

DANNY TWISTED THE CAP off the green Heineken bottle and tossed it into the recycling bin near the door to the lanai.

He had made a few minor adjustments to the outside of the house since moving in—a coat of paint here, a plant there—but for the most part, it was the same as when Lynn Shields lived in it.

He thought back to the morning of his shooting and about how close he'd come to dying—dying in a way that was much different from the way Lynn Shields did, perhaps, but dying was dying. Sarah's investigative spirit and Tracy's recounting of childhood stories were the only reasons he was alive. Had they not come looking for him, who knows when someone would have eventually made it out to the beach?

It had been over a year now, and his shoulder still hurt like hell. The doctors had told him it would likely hurt forever, and, à propos of that fateful morning, even more so when it rained.

The police had questioned Danny for a couple hours in the hospital about the injury, but he'd simply told them he couldn't remember anything that happened. Call it amnesia, or whatever, but he had no recollection of how he got to the beach or anything about a shooting. Thankfully, his friends had found him there in that condition, and the bullet had been kind to miss any major organs or arteries. The last thing he remembered was leaving his home to meet up with them for an early breakfast, and he wound up face down in the sand on Rove Beach. Must have been a mugging gone wrong.

There was no weapon, of course, and no descriptions of suspects, which meant there wasn't much to go on as far as cracking the case. There were a few follow-up interviews, which Danny participated in voluntarily, but, of course, nothing new was revealed from those either.

Lynn Shields' disappearance, the part of the story Danny had assumed would be the biggest obstacle in the cover up, wasn't much of one at all.

"Hey Danny." Tracy opened the screen door and walked out to the lanai, tossing a towel on the chaise and opening a bottle of sunscreen. "You coming out to the beach today?"

Lynn Shields' house had been left to Tracy in her will, but Danny's subsequent offer to purchase it had involved too much for Tracy to turn down, both in terms of cash and conditions. For her home, Danny had paid almost one and a half times the appraised price. And, so that the real details surrounding Lynn Shields' death remained a secret, Tracy was allowed to live in the home rent-free. And, in the event of Danny's death, whenever that occurred, the house would be returned back to her.

It was perfect.

There was also the issue of Tammy's disappearance, but Danny had no answers for that either. The two of them were having problems in their marriage, he lied, so it wasn't impossible she'd simply left. Maybe the whole 'Rove Beach Monster' thing had gotten to her, and she couldn't deal with his obsession anymore. He didn't know. She just left one day and never came back. It happened. That lie he'd even told to Sarah, and though her suspicion was palpable, she never questioned him about it anymore.

Danny thought about his interviews with the police on each of these matters, and despite their suspicion of him and his involvement in at least one of these mysteries, they never once questioned the validity of the creature and the pictures he'd taken. Why wouldn't they at least consider the possibility that it was real?

He thought of Tammy again. He rarely spoke of her anymore, as even now it was a painful memory to vocalize. But he thought about her constantly, paying particular attention to the dark morning of her death.

When he'd first witnessed the glory of the God.

By Danny's calculations, tonight was the first night of the new cycle. Sarah would be arriving for dinner soon to attend the trio's monthly get together.

And the grotto was ready.

Sarah would be offered tonight, Danny decided, and Tracy would go tomorrow. The sedatives had already been diluted into the wine.

He would try to find one more before the week was out. Prostitutes were exceptionally easy to find only a few miles outside of town. Or maybe he'd offer that jarhead Mark—no doubt he'd be poking around in a few days looking for his gal.

Would a week be too long? Would the God move on if he didn't feed it consistently after the first night? If it did, Danny would have to wait for another cycle. Another fourteen months.

But he would wait. And learn. Just as Lynn did.

Danny walked to the dunes and sifted through the beach grass, his fingers finding the stiff Play button of the nineties-era boombox. He pushed it until it clicked into position, and then stood tall, listening to the mating call of the minke whales as he stared out over the Atlantic.

THE END

About the Author

CHRISTOPHER COLEMAN lives in Maryland with his wife and two children. He is a graduate of the University of Maryland with a degree in English Literature. A fan of classic and modern horror and thriller movies, his favorite movies are Rosemary's Baby and The Ring. When he's not writing fiction, you can find him reading, taking his kids to and from various sporting activities or watching horror movies with his wife who shares his affinity for the horror genre. His books will creep you out and leave you scared to turn off the lights and go to sleep.

Subscribe to Christopher Coleman's Newsletter

HTTP://WWW.CHRISTOPHERCOLEMANAU-THOR.com/newsletter/[1]

---

1. http://www.christophercolemanauthor.com/newsletter/

Leave a review for The Sighting

https://www.amazon.com/Sighting-Suspenseful-Mystery-Horror-Thriller-ebook/dp/B076MJ5GVC/

More from Christopher Coleman

Gretel (Gretel Book One)[1]
Marlene's Revenge (Gretel Book Two)[2]
Hansel (Gretel Book Three)[3]
Anika Rising (Gretel Book Four)[4]
They Came with the Snow[5]

---

1. https://www.amazon.com/Gretel-Book-One-Christopher-Coleman-ebook/dp/B01605OOL4/

2. https://www.amazon.com/Marlenes-Revenge-Gretel-Book-Two-ebook/dp/B01LX8R3LD/

3. https://www.amazon.com/Hansel-Gretel-Book-Three-Suspenseful-ebook/dp/B072L8C5SN/

4. https://www.amazon.com/Anika-Rising-Gretel-Book-Four-ebook/dp/B0784MXFHD/

5. https://www.amazon.com/They-Came-Snow-Christopher-Coleman-ebook/dp/B06XPL2Q4L/

Sample from Gretel (Gretel Book One)
CHAPTER ONE

SHE'D NEVER GOTTEN used to the taste. Even with the life and strength that teemed in every molecule, the russet fluid always went down heavy and crude. Like swallowing a fistful of thin mud that had been lifted from the bottom of a river.

There was a time in the early years of her life—this second life—when she was forced to mix the liquid with soup or tea, or to stir it into the batter of the sweet confections and pies that even today she took pleasure in baking. She had experimented relentlessly with temperatures and combinations—using ingredients she wouldn't have otherwise fed to a cockroach—hoping to create a formula that, if not tasty, was at least palatable enough to override the involuntary rejection by her mouth and throat.

But she'd had little success, and soon began believing the more she tampered with and diluted the delicate recipe, the more the regenerative effects were diminished. Her nails and hair didn't seem to grow quite as quickly, and her teeth, though they were restored, felt as if they had just a bit less length and severity.

Of course, it was plausible she was entirely wrong about the effects of the tampering, and she accepted the possibility that her observations were paranoid inventions of an overprotective mind. But she also wasn't taking any chances, and over time she had trained herself to drink the mixture straight. After all, it took mere seconds for the solution to make it over her taste buds and down to her belly. After that, it was ecstasy.

The mixture usually began its rolling boil within seconds of reaching the acid that lined her stomach, before shooting into her blood stream and picking up the platelets in perfect stride. From there the journey through the body took less than a minute, administering almost instant relief to pains both bitter and dormant alike. There was a sense of rejuvenation in the bones and ligaments that went beyond simply where they joined. It was cellular.

The feeling in those first few moments was literally indescribable. On the rare occasions she had tried to explain it aloud, she always found there was simply no adequate experience with which to compare it. The benchmark didn't exist. Sex—usually the standard by which all great feelings were measured—didn't come close. Though it had been decades since she'd had a man, and in her lifetime had little experience with them generally, she knew even with the greatest lover in history, sex was a laughable comparison. As was the feeling elicited by any other potion, and potions she knew. What she lacked in bedroom prowess, she made up for in a long resume of chemical experiences.

But the physical feeling, as glorious as it was, was inconsequential. A minor side effect of the greatest treasure the Old World had ever produced, and one that she had captured and preserved in the Northlands for centuries. Whether she alone was in possession of the knowledge she couldn't be sure; it certainly wasn't impossible that another had been given the precious gift to which she had clung so tightly for the last three hundred years. But if she did share it with another, she would likely never know; her isolation had become almost absolute. The Age of Transmission had transformed her existence from that of a private villager—having few social connections other than in passing and commercial exchanges—to one of complete withdrawal. There were no neighbors to speak of, and any mail or necessary supplies were delivered to the receiving station she had built for herself just over a half-mile from the cabin.

The woman picked up the large, stone container and swirled the liquid into a clockwise vortex, careful not to lose any of it over the top—though caution was mostly unnecessary, since what remained of the potable would have fit easily into a jigger.

This sip was different, however, and her careful attention was not without cause. This swig was the last of her batch. It was the final priceless ounce. She knew in her core it wasn't really enough for full revitalization; it would replenish for another year if she limited her energy, even two if she did nothing but sleep. After that she would decline quickly. And since the elixir didn't spare her from the necessary provisions of all human beings—food, heat, and so on—languidness and hibernation were no more a possibility for her than they were for the woman she was in her old life. In fact, she would need to exert more energy than most people, since she was not surrounded by the accommodations of a modern world. She would need to farm and gather, and even hunt if the harvest didn't last through winter, as well as keep an ample supply of kindling and wood. And she wasn't the youngest maiden in the court when she began the regimen—certainly past sixty years as she recalled—so though the potion sustained her and kept her strong, what was done was done: the contaminations of time did not reverse.

The woman raised the stone cup, which was little more than a small bowl, careful not to breathe the rancid aroma. As it reached her lips, the woman hesitated. This was it, she thought, this last drink would drain her supply, leaving her cabin empty of the fluid she'd come to worship over the many decades.

She willed a pragmatic moment into her addicted mind. Maybe she could hold out for a few months longer. Just a few, until she identified the source of her next supply. There really wasn't the urgency to drink today, she still felt strong and capable. Why, just this morning she had restocked the wood pile after several hours of brisk chopping. And besides, it had only been fourteen months since her last dose. Certainly she had gone without for much longer.

All of that was true. But the reality was that the effects had diminished over the years, and she needed larger doses now than in the past. As it was, her last drink had been meager, having been divided in half to leave today's swallow. No, she needed it today, all of it, and if it was enough to sustain her until the end of summer, she would be lucky. The woman figured by June she would need to be blending.

She pinched her nose and drank slowly, relaxing the pharyngeal nerve at the back of her throat to prevent gagging. The sickening warmth lingered on her soft palate, and then descended the length of her windpipe. The woman could feel the pulp of her victims organs catch and then release in her esophagus, and she lamented that, although she'd always spent days pestling, she had never been able to thin out the concoction completely. This part had always been the hardest—in the early days often inducing violent spasms of choking and expectoration. What she had coughed up over the years! The amount could have sustained her for another generation.

But those reactions had subsided long ago; aside from the taste, she had mostly gotten used to the process. Like the gypsy sword swallowers she had seen as a girl, so nonchalantly on the backs of their wagons immersing those giant blades, inconceivably, down into their bellies and back up again, before packing up and quietly moving on to the next village, she had learned to ingest the pungent broth with little effort.

But there was still the taste. She could never get used to the taste.

She placed the ceramic cup on the edge of the cast iron stove and gently walked to the lone wooden chair that occupied her kitchen. She sat wide-eyed and rigid on the edge of the seat, anticipating the impending experience of which she never tired. Then the slight hint of a bubble began in her abdomen, and a smile formed on the ancient woman's face.

WHEN SHE AWOKE IT WAS just before dawn, and she could hear the first whistling of the woodcocks as they began to pester the sun. Spring had arrived weeks ago, but the chill of the morning stung the back of her neck and prompted an exaggerated shiver. She reached instinctively for covering, and instead created finger tracks in the thick dust of the wooden floor. She grasped her hand again in a slight panic and was now quickly awake.

This wasn't the first time she had gone black—it had happened several times over the years—but those incidences had occurred mostly in the beginning, and never lasted this long, apparently, judging by the position of the sun, almost a full day. She was weaker than she thought, and the truth, which she had numbed her mind to, was that the mixture was old and diminished. Perhaps even toxic. She thought back to when the batch was originally concocted but couldn't recall. Forty years perhaps? Certainly well past the period for which she could reasonably expect it to remain fully viable. What if it had become inert and didn't deliver the effects this time? That seemed unlikely, since the immediate burn and thrill in her abdomen was just as magnificent as ever, but the unusual side effect of unconsciousness suggested a serious problem.

She tried to stand and was prostrated to the floor by a stab of lightning to her back. In disbelief, the old woman tried again, this time using the seat of the chair as a crutch. She was able to rise to her knees before the pain delivered another bolt. A scream attempted to escape her mouth but was immediately intercepted by phlegm and sickness. She laid her forehead on the chair and took deep, panicked breaths. It hadn't worked! This couldn't be happening! She lifted her head and glanced frantically around the room searching for the empty stone cup, hoping beyond reason that whatever trace amounts remained at the bottom of the urn would somehow be enough to release the magic. Maybe one last drop was all she needed.

She spotted the cup. It had rolled to the door of the cabin, the rim edging against the jamb as if waiting to be let out. She got down on all fours and crawled slowly toward the door, exaggerating every lift of her knees for fear of the returning agony to her back.

The woman reached the cup, took a deep, labored breath, and assumed a sitting position, leaning her back against the door for support. She sat that way for several moments until her breathing slowed and her thoughts leveled, and then closed her eyes in an extended blink. She then lifted the cup gently, cradling it from the bottom with both hands as if preparing to offer it in sacrifice, all the time feeling its cruel emptiness. She didn't bother to look inside, and instead placed the cup softly beside her before pushing herself forward and resting tall on her knees.

She closed her eyes again and bowed her head, thankful for the clarity that had presented itself. Her survival would not be dependent on whatever residue remained at the bottom. It would take faith and action. It was time again to accept what is and move on.

Of all the lessons she had learned in her long life, this one had come most grudgingly. But it *had* come, eventually, and once she embraced it, once she'd moved beyond just repeating the words to herself and had finally felt the power and truth of the phrase, it had been the greatest lesson of all. In the past, her reaction to this ruined batch of potion would likely have sent her into some uncontrolled rampage, screaming maniacally for hours, cursing the universe and destroying what few possessions she had. And then, once the fury subsided, she would conclude the episode by erupting into wild tears of self-pity, and then spending the rest of her precious day thinking of suicide and vengeful murder.

But that was in the past. Those futile thoughts of injustice and revenge were pollution to her mind and, for decades, had only weakened her. They were antithetical to what Life craved. She was still somewhat envious of those who had come to realize this fact in the span of a normal lifetime, but she was thankful it had eventually come to her. And thankful for her secret of immortality.

"I'll find it," she said softly.

She lifted her chin and stared out the window, as the sun's first rays provided just enough backlight to silhouette the multitude of lush trees that formed the spring forest. It was going to be a beautiful day. The sky would be clear, and the cool nip of the morning promised relief from the unseasonably warm days of the past week. It was perhaps a harbinger of a new start, she thought. The pain had vanished from her back, and her mind was as clear and unpolluted as ice. And silent. She reveled in the stillness, allowing every sensation of the surroundings to wash over her and soak into her skin. Yes, it was time to begin anew.

The old woman smiled widely, unleashing the large, jagged incisors and canines that crowded the front of her mouth. They were in need of replacement, but they were serviceable.

She stood from her kneeling position and walked to the makeshift wardrobe that anchored the rear wall of the small cottage. The wonder of faith now overwhelmed her, and she had no doubt that renewal loomed. It was only a matter of time—though time was leaking.

She removed the only piece of clothing that hung from one of a dozen wooden hooks that lined the back of the wardrobe's interior. The garment was a moth-ridden wool cloak, heavy and dark—a piece of clothing designed for frost and survival, from an era harsh and bygone. She placed the coat effortlessly over her torso and raised the oversized hood. She would undoubtedly be uncomfortable while the sun was up, since the day was likely to be warm and dry. But the cloak would protect her skin, which had become sensitive to direct sunlight—a thing she rarely received through the canopy of the forest—and if she were forced to camp overnight, the wool would keep her warm in the evening chill.

But such an adventure shouldn't be necessary, she thought. There was still time. Perhaps plenty of time. Going black was simply a sign that her moment had come to awaken and begin identifying the fresh source. To reconnoiter the landscape for the new point of supply. She had done it dozens of times since that first night so long ago, and, in fact, had become quite adept at tracking viable sources.

But identifying meant travel, a practice about which she had always been anxious and leery. Even as a young woman, before the Discovery, the unknown wilderness had always invoked feelings of dread and tragedy. By seven or eight years of age, her mother had so often explained the seemingly unlimited evils of men that she couldn't imagine any woman stepping off her property without being raped or beaten or enslaved. And she soon learned that the tales, though perhaps exaggerated, weren't simply cautionary. She had seen the truth of them first hand, and, indeed, had performed many of the cruel acts herself. Had those women she tortured been as cautious as she, they would have not been in that position, she often rationalized.

Yes, it was the quality of caution that had served her well and preserved her existence since The Enlightenment. But as always, caution was always overruled by necessity. It was time once again to hunt.

She stepped down gingerly onto the crude stone landing that served as a porch and settled for a moment without moving. She listened as a distant breeze pushed through the green of the forest, moving deliberately past each leaf and limb, before finally catching her in its wake. Yes, this would be a fine day. She lowered the cloak's hood, deciding she would begin the journey exposed to the wonders of the woods, figuring the sun would not be a factor for several miles, and the chances of encountering another person were remote.

She took another step on the porch and immediately recognized the adrenaline that had surged during her earlier moment of clarity was now waning. She could already feel the weakness of her joints and muscles returning. The sting of old age, a feeling she had forgotten, or perhaps never known, billowed down her spine and limbs, and the pain choked in a breath as she tried to exhale. Alarmed, she moved quickly toward the edge of the porch, convincing herself that by reaching the boardwalk at the bottom of the steps and beginning her journey on the overgrown pathway that led into the forest, she could somehow outpace the inevitable.

She reached the ledge of the stairs, barely, her legs giving out on the last stride, and narrowly avoided tumbling to the bottom. Only the stone wall that bordered the descent saved her from catastrophe. She held the barrier in a comic clutch, as if trying to keep a battleship from leaving port, and looked out at the seemingly endless timberland before her. She laughed aloud at the idea of venturing ten yards from home, let alone the ten miles or so it would require to reach the nearest source population. It was impossible. And rest was not the answer. Rest meant time and time meant decay. What the woman needed was help, and help—even more than companionship—had always been the greatest price of her isolation. The lack of companionship, or even the sound of an-other's voice, could certainly be brutal realities, but there were ways to deal with those. She had come to consider the trees and animals and insects important companions in her life and addressed them with respect and appreciation. And she had long since shed any embarrassment of speaking aloud or taking on dif-ferent character roles. This, in fact—along with her baking—had become one of the few joys in her life, invoking the characteristics of women from her past that she had always envied or admired, playing the roles of huntress or princess or whore. Early on she had discovered that for even the most primal of human relationships there were always alternatives, as any thirteen-year-old boy could attest to.

But there was no substitute for the strength of men to remove an old iron stove, or fell a dying tree before it collapsed and demolish a house. Or for hands to help gather and hunt when the crops have failed and starvation is no further than a bad snowstorm away. She had paid for help in the past—and even kept slaves when the social climate allowed it—and though these servants had cer-tainly alleviated many of the normal personal and practical burdens, the threat of loss had been too strong, and they never stayed on for long. Most of them she killed while they slept. Many were buried on this very property. Sadly, none of their innards were used for blending.

And now isolation would cost her immortality. The motif of so many leg-ends and religions would evaporate with her last breath, as it may have done, for all she knew, with hundreds of other possessive hermits in the past.

She lowered herself down to a sitting position on the first step of the porch and rested her elbows on her knees. She coughed several times as if she had just finished a brisk winter walk and her lungs were struggling to adjust. She hung her head between her knees and watched as the wooden planks beneath her be-gan to blur. She was about to go black again, perhaps permanently this time. Instinctively, she slid her buttocks to the next step down and continued this movement on to each lower tread until she reached the bottom. If she were go-ing to die, she decided, it wouldn't be from a broken neck. There was one last impulse to get to her feet, but the message was never conveyed from her brain to her legs. Defeated, the old woman rolled onto her back and spread her arms wide, encouraging the world's embrace. She took in the bright blueness of the sky and wished that she could feel the wonder of rain one last time.

The blue canvas above her turned shadowy, not from the arrival of clouds, she assumed, but from her brain's lack of oxygen. She smelled the warm air rising from the ground, and tried to appreciate the last of life's sensory experiences. Surely this was death. She had escaped it for so long, but now here it was in front of her. The brew of life on which she had relied since the early times of the Northlands had finally failed her. Or she had failed it. It was true she trusted a source would come—her dreams had told her of its delivery—but it hadn't come, and she'd waited too long to move on. She'd trusted in her dreams and they had betrayed her, but it was *her* life, *her* responsibility. She had become careless and complacent. The supply was larger than ever these days, and she needed only to pull from it.

If only there was more time. A week. A day.

"I'm sorry," she whispered. "I'm sorry." She closed her eyes and slowed her breathing, as that relentless resistance to death which had dictated the bulk of her life now turned to acceptance. Without contention, she awaited sleep.

And then she heard the voice.

ANIKA MORGAN WAS COLD, and the mud that had gently cushioned the soles of her feet when she set out now enveloped her ankles and threatened to swallow her shins. Every step felt like someone was pressing down on the tops of her knees. She thought of quicksand. Was that a possibility? That this was quicksand? She knew—or at least had heard the stories as a child—about quicksand existing in the jungles of Africa and places like that, but not in the Northlands. Truthfully though, she couldn't be sure where it was found. Or if it was real at all. Was she really going to die such an improbable death as drowning in quicksand?

Anika cleared her head and focused. If she wanted to avoid death today, she figured it wasn't quicksand she had to worry about. Besides, quicksand was absurd, the forests of this territory were infamous for their swamps and mud; she had waded through much worse in her life. She had to stay on task.

"Just go," she scolded herself.

She wanted to scream the words, but her overworked lungs wouldn't allow it. Anika slowed her breathing and down-shifted her effort to an easy walk. The depth of the mud was making her progress comically slow, and trying to run through it was doing nothing but edging her closer to exhaustion. Adrenaline had its limits, and hers was almost reached. She would have to rest soon. In a few hours, the early morning chill would be giving way to the warmth of a typical spring day, and Anika could see the sun beginning its morning stretch upward. The sky was almost staggering in its clarity and blueness, and she was thankful at least to be dry; though had it been raining, she reasoned, she would never have attempted the forest to begin with, and probably would have been rescued by now.

But she *had* chosen the forest, and at the time had done so quite casually.

But why?

Why would she have made such an unconventional decision? Such a bad decision? She was normally much more conservative in her approach to problems, and the woods in this country, even on a clear spring day, were risky to explore for the most well-conditioned of men, let alone a thirty-eight-year-old mother of two. So why hadn't she just walked the road? Or waited for help at the place where the car drifted off the shoulder? It was true she wasn't thinking clearly after the accident—everything had happened so quickly—but she hadn't suffered any trauma to her head. In fact, she was miraculously uninjured.

So the question remained: why?

It didn't matter now, she thought, the decision was made; all that mattered now was finding shelter and a telephone. Besides, with her car nestled at the bottom of what must have been a fifteen-foot embankment, with little hope of being seen from the road, it seemed somewhat reasonable that finding a place to call for help on her own was a safer play than standing alone on the side of a quiet road in the southern Northlands. Not that this part of the territory was particularly dangerous, but one could never be sure.

Anika spotted a log about forty yards in the distance and decided it would be a suitable place to rest. She wanted to keep going, but she knew forty yards was about all she had left in her. If she pushed beyond that, she might not come across another place to stop, and would end up having to rest in the mud she was desperately trying to escape.

And she was getting scared. And fear, she knew, would only make her judgment worse.

She needed to stop and think, try to orient herself with what little she knew of the land here, and get out of these woods and back to her family. She could only imagine the fears they would conjure if they didn't hear from her soon. She should have been home by now, and it wouldn't be long before they started to worry. Soon they would call to check on her and learn that she had left ahead of schedule and should have been home even earlier. And that would be bad. She loved Heinrich, but for all his pretensions of strength and masculinity, he was emotionally weak. And combined with his injuries, he would be in no condition to comfort and reassure the children.

She reached the large log and climbed atop to a sitting position, throwing one muddy leg to the far side to straddle it. She sat this way for a moment, legs dangling while she caught her breath, and finally lay down on her back, bringing her legs together and linking her hands behind her head for support. Under the circumstances, it felt strange to be assuming such a relaxed position, and she imagined that someone looking in might conclude that she was on some spiritual journey—albeit one that was oddly messy—and had come to the forest to contemplate the meaning of life or something.

If only.

It was still early and she'd only been up a few hours, but the grueling hike had tired Anika and she had to be mindful to stay awake. She had to keep her eyes wide and her mind active. She thought of her children and how they must miss her. She realized now it was the longest she had ever been away from them, only a little over a week, but it was eons compared to what they were used to, and, with Heinrich in his condition, it came at a time when she was needed at home most. They were both wonderful, mature children, exceptional for their ages, but they had no business carrying the responsibilities she had left them with this past week. Why hadn't she just waited by the road?

Anika sat straight on the log and took the last remaining bite of a stale candy bar. It had been in her car for days—weeks maybe—and she was thrilled now to have grabbed it before setting out. At least she'd made one good decision today.

She swallowed the chocolate and then laid back down to fully replenish her lungs and examine her options. She supposed she could try to retrace her steps and get back to the original point where she had entered the forest, and then wait on the shoulder of the road until someone passed by. The roads were certainly desolate on the stretch where she'd swerved off—in fact, she couldn't re-member passing a car once in her short trip from Father's house—but surely someone would eventually motor by and help. Even if it took several hours. At this point, the fear of some lascivious stranger with devious motives paled to the fear she had of still being in these woods come nightfall.

But the truth was it was too late for the road, at least at the part where her car now lay abandoned and invisible. Whatever it was that had compelled her into the wilderness had now taken her beyond the point where she had the will to make it back. It would be a disheartening trek of over an hour through the now detestable mud, and at this point she wasn't sure she would even be able to find it. The turns she had made along the way to avoid the deeper swampy areas and larger thickets had disoriented Anika, and though she was fairly confident that she could head back in the general direction she had come, with fatigue and fear now a factor, there was no certainty she would reach the road at all.

Her other option—only option really—was to continue on. She realized she may only immerse herself deeper, but eventually she would reach a bound-ary. This was the Northlands, not the Amazon, after all. She had to keep going and cling to the fact that possibility rested in every new clearing.

She stood up on the log and slowly surveyed the forest in each direction, hoping by some wonder of the universe her eyes would focus past the camou-flage and spot something other than trees. It wasn't a particularly dense wood-land, so even with the lush spring leaves there was quite a bit of visibility. But she saw nothing. She jumped down off the log and searched the forest again, this time at ground level, figuring she may have more luck at a different an-gle. Nothing. She climbed the log again and this time stood tall, straighten-ing her back, and cupped her mouth with her hands. She breathed deeply and screamed as loudly as possible.

"Help me! Can anybody hear me!"

The words seemed to float through the trees, echoing off the branches and carrying downwind. With the additional height of the log, her voice felt force-ful, and the decision to yell now seemed less an act of desperation and more of an actual rescue strategy. She paused and listened, not expecting a response, and, of course, getting none. She screamed again, this time feeling a strained burn in her throat. She couldn't remember ever having yelled this loud as an adult. Still nothing, and the subsequent silence was stark, only reinforcing her desertion. She couldn't know that the sound waves of this particular bellow deflected at just the proper angle, avoiding perfectly the large oak trunks and dense clumps of leaves that should have absorbed them forever, traveling instead just far enough from their source to reach the auditory canal of an old woman who lay dying on a weathered terrace less than four miles away.

Anika moved down to a sitting position on the log, broke off a dying branch, and began clearing as much mud as possible from her shoes and pant cuffs. It was a futile exercise she knew—they'd be covered again in a matter of paces—but she needed whatever boost she could get. At least she hadn't worn a dress today, she thought. It could always be worse.

She placed her feet back down on the damp dirt floor and was startled by a rustle beneath the log. She stifled a gasp and watched as two chipmunks ran past her and headed up a nearby tree. Anika unconsciously cataloged the vermin as a potential food source; though if it came to that, how she would trap such small, fleeting creatures she had no idea. She watched the tiny animals disappear into the camouflage of the tree's top branches and then continued her upward gaze to the clear blue sky. It was indeed a marvelous day, she thought, and then she started walking.

THE OLD WOMAN OPENED her eyes and searched her surroundings with the vibrancy of an infant seeing the world for the first time. The voice was faint—perhaps the faintest sound she had ever heard—but that she had heard it there was no doubt. It may be the voice of Death, she thought, but if it was, he was incarnate. That sound had come in through her ears, not her imagination. She replayed the words in her mind. Over and over. The voice was feminine—beautiful and distressed. Strong. Alive. Not the voice of Death. The voice of Life. Delivering again.

CHAPTER TWO

"ANIKA!"

Gretel Morgan flinched violently at the sound of her father's voice, somehow managing not to drop the ceramic plate she had been drying over the sink. He was awake, and, as was usually the case lately, unhappy.

"It's me, Father, I'll be right there," she called, turning her head slightly toward the back bedroom, trying her best not to sound aggravated. She certainly sympathized with his condition but had grown tired of the demands it came with.

Gretel sighed and placed the dish on the sideboard. She had hoped to finish the cleaning before he woke since her tasks seemed to multiply when he was conscious. Cooking his meals alone was a day's work; add in laundering his clothes (including ironing) and general fetching, and the assignment was barbaric. Thankfully, Mother would be home today, at least to bear some of the constant attention, if not the heavy lifting.

Gretel walked the ten or so paces to her father's room and paused at the door, softly clearing her throat and assuming the statuesque, confident posture her mother always seemed to have when she entered a room. At fourteen, her shoulders and hips had begun to forge, and early indications suggested she would have her mother's shapely body. She had no delusions of striding in and conquering her father's petulance in the same effortless way her mother did, of course, but hopefully she could disarm him if only for a moment.

She formed what she believed was a serious, business-like look on her face and entered the room. She could see that her father was sitting up slightly in his bed, but avoided his eyes and walked briskly to the end table, feigning irritation at the crumbs and empty glasses that littered its surface.

"Where is your mother?" her father grumbled, his deep, accented speech at once both intimidating and divine. "She was to be home by now."

"She's probably not coming home," Gretel replied casually, letting the words drift just to the edge of uneasiness. "I wouldn't blame her. If I was her I would have changed my name and run away to a village in the south." She kept her eyes down, serious, staying excessively focused on her father's mess.

Her father frowned and stared coldly at his daughter. "Perhaps I'll send you to a village in the south."

Gretel stopped sponging the table in mid-motion, and stared up at her father with a look of both disbelief and anticipation. "Would you? Please! Promise me, Papa!" She held his gaze for as long as possible before losing control of the charade and erupting into a snorted laugh.

Her father shook his head slowly and grinned. Gretel could see the flicker of joy in his eyes, proud of how quick his daughter had become with her banter. Yet another gift inherited from her mother.

"How are you feeling, Papa?" Gretel said, now straight-faced, unable to conceal her weariness. She sat on the edge of the bed and examined her father's bandages.

"Better than I look."

"Well, you look terrible."

"So better than terrible then." He waved an absent hand and began shuffling to get on his feet, having reached the extent of how much he wanted to discuss himself or his maladies. "Get me up."

"You need to stay in bed, Papa. You're not ready."

"Then you had better be ready with the piss pot."

With that, Gretel stooped and leaned in toward her father, offering her shoulder as a crutch. She could see him size up her position, and with a soft, guttural grunt he threw an arm around his daughter's neck, embarrassment no longer the palpable element it had been six weeks ago. His white bedshirt was badly stained with some type of red sauce, and his ever-growing belly extended over the elastic of his tattered long underpants. It had amazed Gretel the short time it took for a man with such a long-standing trademark of pride and masculinity to concede to the often cruel circumstances of life; in the case of her father, those circumstances had come most recently in the form of three fractured ribs—not exactly the bubonic plague in the hierarchy of ailments, but painfully debilitating nevertheless. Particularly for a man nearing sixty.

Gretel boosted him from the bed and shuffled him slowly to the threshold of the washroom, grimacing throughout the process, and from there left him to his own maneuvers. The doctor had explained to her mother that the injury would likely cause a decrease in appetite, since even automatic bodily functions like swallowing and digesting could be painful, and limited activity would reduce his need for the same amount of nourishment he was getting before the accident. The opposite, however, was proving true; he ate constantly and, as a result, had become quite heavy. She couldn't be sure, but Gretel guessed that her father had gained at least forty pounds in little over a month.

"So where is your mother?" The voice from behind the bathroom door was less demanding now and contained the subtle hint of concern. Gretel had lingered outside since she would have to bring her father back when he was done.

"Delayed, I guess. But she must have left Deda's already or else she would have telephoned."

"Then why didn't she phone to say she would be delayed?" His pitch was now higher and layered with obstinance.

"Perhaps she was delayed on the road, I don't know Papa." She paused and asked, "Are you going to be in there much longer?" Gretel was now annoyed, both at her father for his current weakness and at her mother for being late. There were still dishes remaining in the kitchen, and she needed a break—if only for fifteen minutes—to sit and rest. Not working or helping or talking. Just to rest.

"Maybe you should bathe," she suggested, offering the words in the tone of a helpful reminder so as not to offend him. "You'll call Deda's when you're out." Her father mumbled something inaudible from behind the door, and then a grain of joy arose in Gretel at the abrupt sound of water being released from the tub's faucet.

She sighed with relief and walked back toward the kitchen, her desire to finish housework now dwarfed by the urge to rest. She averted her gaze from the sink as she passed it, and headed quickly for the back porch, where she collapsed forcefully in a white, weathered rocker. She tilted her face up toward the ceiling and closed her eyes, thankful for the chance to relax, but understanding that what she really needed was sleep. Sleep had now become the default thought in her mind throughout the day, and, in fact, had become of such value since her father's accident, that over the past three weeks Gretel had started her mornings by staring at herself in the small nightstand mirror by her bed and listing in her mind the things that she would be willing to give up for an undisturbed day of slumber. A full day. Not one chore. Not one knock. Not even a voice. Just complete serenity. Of course, she possessed virtually nothing of her own, so this exercise basically involved the sacrifices of treasures she would never see and powers she would never have, the latest offering being a horse that could fly. Later, in the throes of the day, she would scoff at how little value she would have gotten from her imagined trade-offs; but she was convinced that, at the time, she would have made the deal.

Gretel could feel herself drifting, and decided not to fight. The dishes remained, but her mother would be home soon, and though she would be in no mood to finish her daughter's chores after a long day of travel, Gretel concluded that as a parent she would recognize when her child was spent. If her father needed help back to his bed she would help, but aside from that, she was done for the day.

"SHE'S NOT HOME, GRETEL."

Gretel opened her eyes and was greeted by the orange glow of the twilight sky above her. She was momentarily disoriented, but smelled the oil from the lamps and remembered she was on the porch. Her late afternoon catnap had metastasized into solid sleep. By her estimation, she was out for at least four hours.

Her thoughts immediately went to her father, whom, for all she knew, was in the tub dead, a victim of immobility, hypothermia, and a neglectful daughter.

She got up quickly from the rocker and felt the effect of her sleeping position in the form of a dull stiffness at the back of her neck. No question she would be dealing with that misery for the rest of the night. Tentatively, Gretel turned back toward the house and screamed at the sight of her father sitting at the porch table, dressed and shaven, his elbows propped up and his head buried in his hands. He looked as if her were in a library reading—the way one might read a dictionary or an atlas—but there was nothing on the table below him.

Her initial thoughts were of relief, that her father was alive and that she was not a murderer. Then, registering his condition, her thoughts became more selfish, assuming his apparent improvement meant she would now get real relief. Physical relief. More sleep.

She stood staring at him, waiting for him to speak, but he sat in position, silent.

"Papa?" she said, "What's wrong?" Gretel spoke softly, but her tone had no sympathy and was one demanding an explanation. Her father didn't move and she became uneasy, then scared. "What's wrong!" she said again, this time louder, panicked and quivery, the film of sleep and the surreality of her father sitting upright in a chair on the porch, functional, now completely wiped away.

"She's not home, Gretel." Her father lifted his head from his hands and looked out through the trees at the small narrow lake that lined their property.

Gretel could see where the tears had been on his freshly-washed cheeks and she noted that this was as close to weeping as she'd ever seen from either of her parents.

"Something's happened," he said, "I know something's happened."

Her father's words caused Gretel's legs to wobble, and she sat back down slowly in the rocker. She couldn't speak, and looked off in the same direction as her father, as if they were both trying to spot the same object on the water. "Did you call Deda?" she asked finally, in a whisper, already knowing the answer.

"Of course I called him. She left even earlier than she had told me she would. She should have been home long before we expected her." There was no anger in her father's voice, only defeat.

"Perhaps there was traffic then. A very bad accident...and the road is closed."

"I've called The System. There is no report of any accident along the Interways."

Gretel could hear in her father's tone that the bases had been covered. Heinrich Morgan was a man of routine, as was his wife, and any break from that routine would immediately incite him to make it right again. To look at all the possibilities and rule them out, one by one, until the answer to the problem emerged. And if the remaining answers were out of his control, and he couldn't reset the routine to its proper function, he shut down. This was the point he had apparently reached.

The tears in Gretel's eyes seemed to be dripping to the floor before she even felt the sadness, and her face flushed with hate for her father's weakness. Nothing was wrong! Her mother was fine! He should be ashamed, a grown man crying in front of his teenage daughter because her mother is a few hours late. For a month he had contributed nothing to the house—NOTHING—other than dirty plates and whines of discomfort. Gretel and her mother had worked the fields for six weeks while he moaned over a few broken bones in his belly. If only that horse had kicked his head! And now, when strength was needed—when he was needed—he was a clammy dishrag, like a woman who's just watched her son leave for war.

Gretel erupted from the rocking chair and ran toward her room, ignoring the sharp pain that burned through her neck the whole way. She stumbled in and fell face down on the foot end of her bed, nearly crashing her head on the bench of the small white vanity that sat only inches away. Almost immediately, she stood back up and strode defiantly back to the open bedroom door, slamming it harder than she thought she was capable of. For that split moment she felt better than she could remember in weeks, as if the suppressed grievances of her fourteen-year-old body and mind were instantly alleviated.

She went back to her bed and took a more conventional position, curled fetal-like at the head with her cheek flat on the quilt cover.

The heavy sobs finally ended and Gretel lay still until her crying stopped completely. She rolled to her back and gazed vacuously at the brown wood that made up the cabin ceiling. Her thoughts became clear as she studied the evidence of the situation and soon became hopeful. This is all certainly an overreaction, she thought. Papa's condition has unsettled him and I've let it influence me. There's a good chance—better than good—that Mother is completely fine. In fact, there was a much higher likelihood that her mother was stranded on the road somewhere waiting for help to arrive, than lying dead on a river bank or in a landfill. True, she should have been home hours ago—if she left early, then at least six or seven hours to be more accurate—and she had taken the trip up North dozens of times over the past four or five years since Deda had become sick, so she wouldn't have become lost. But none of that evinced tragedy. Gretel reasoned that if something truly terrible had happened, someone would know by now and the family would have been contacted.

But her father's words bore the texture of truth; if not because of the sure somberness of his words—"Something's happened"—than for the possible explanations available. Even if Deda had suddenly been rushed away in an ambulance and died suddenly en route to a hospital (which, of course, hadn't happened since her father had spoken with him earlier), Mother would have called as soon as she reached the hospital. Mother always called. If she didn't call, there was a problem. In this case, Gretel proposed, that problem may simply be a blown tire or some mechanical malfunction in the car. But the Northlands were no more than two hours away on a clear spring day, so it was unlikely she wouldn't have found a telephone by now if it were something so benign. There was no logical reason she could think of that Mother wouldn't have called, other than reasons she didn't want to imagine.

She began to cry again softly, and her mind became overwhelmed with thoughts of never again seeing her mother. It was unimaginable, and physically nauseating. Her mother was everything to her. Everything. Gretel's image of herself as a good young girl—exceptional even—was due solely to the woman she had studied thoroughly and tried for as long as she could remember to emulate. Though Gretel rarely noticed it in the environment which they lived, her mother had a finesse and dignity about her that always astounded Gretel, and only became evident—almost embarrassingly so—when it was contrasted with the tactlessness of most women in the Back Country. She avoided the crude speech that most of the Back Country wives used in an effort somehow to endear themselves to their husbands' friends. Instead she maintained an easy poise that seemed almost regal and out of place. Consequently, of course, her mother stood out among her peers, earning the attention of the men and, Gretel supposed, the backstage scorn of her fellow ladies. She was far from what most people would describe as beautiful, but despite the physical advantages they may have had, other women always appeared intimidated by her mother's confidence.

Gretel got to her feet and walked to the vanity, where she sat on the bench and looked at her distraught face in the mirror as the day's last few rays of sunlight entered her window. It was almost dark and there was no sign of Mother. She turned on the lamp and examined the framed picture of her parents that sat on the vanity top. Her father had gotten very lucky, she thought, and Gretel became sad for him. He was twenty years older than his bride, and in his marriage had always been decided in his ways, insisting on the traditional roles of husband and wife: provider and caregiver, tough and understanding, et cetera.

But in that tradition he had never shown anything but respect and love for her mother. When choices of importance had to be made, concerning her and her brother, or otherwise, Heinrich Morgan always insisted on his wife's opinion. He knew between the two of them she was the smarter one, and he never pretended otherwise.

And though Gretel couldn't remember a time when her father was what she would describe as 'sweet' toward Mother, he certainly never gave her any reason to be docile or frightened around him. He never complained about a meal—whether overcooked or late or for any reason—and he always thanked her when it was over, even offering compliments if he found it exceptional. And if Mother needed to leave him for a day or a week—as in the current situation visiting her ill father—there was never a sense of trepidation when she told him, and the news was always delivered as a statement, with the full expectation that it would be received without protest, if not encouragement. "I'll need to leave for the North tomorrow," her mother would say. "Father's doing poorly. Gretel will handle the house while I'm gone." And father's replies would be nothing other than words of concern for his father-in-law.

The memory of these exchanges suddenly awakened Gretel to the fact that she was not ready to assume this position of authority. The surrogate role of housewife that Gretel had taken on for the last nine days, and that she had begrudgingly admitted to herself was, on some level, enjoyable, was beyond her capabilities. Well beyond. She couldn't do this for five or ten more days let alone years!

Gretel was startled by the muffled sound of the cabin door opening and then closing. She sat motionless, not breathing, and looked at nothing as she shifted her eyes in amazement around the room waiting for the next sound to decipher. Mother! It was definitely Mother. It had to be. Tired and with quite a story to tell, no doubt, but it had to be her. She waited for the booming sound of her father's voice, joyful and scolding, to ring through her room. She wanted to rush out and verify her belief, but she was paralyzed, fearing that somehow by moving she would lose the sound and her hopes would evaporate.

At the tepid knock on her bedroom door, Gretel smiled and lifted herself from the bench, banging her knee on the underside of the vanity and nearly knocking the lamp to the floor, catching it just before it fell. The door cracked and began to open. Gretel looked toward it, waiting for the miracle, holding her awkward lamp-in-hand pose.

It was her father.

"No!" she said, the word erupting from her mouth automatically, denoting both fear and authority, as if she were repelling a spirit that had ventured from hell to inhabit her room. Her father looked at her with sadness and acceptance. "Is she dead?" Gretel said, surprised at the bluntness of her question.

"I don't know, Gretel, we're going to look for her. Your brother is home."

GRETEL LET OUT A RESTRAINED sigh as the family truck pulled in front of her grandfather's small brick house, amazed they had made it. The truck, she guessed, was at least thirty years old, and probably hadn't made a trip this far since before she was born. And each time her father had made one of his dozen or so stops along the way, exploring the considerable land surrounding every curve and potential hazard that the back roads offered, he turned the engine off to conserve fuel. She was sure with each failed effort to locate her mother, the key would click ominously in the ignition when her father tried to restart the engine, and they too would disappear along the road. But it had always started, and here they were.

She looked across the bench seat at her father and was disturbed by the look of indifference on his face. Her brother lay between them asleep.

Her father opened the door and said weakly, "Stay in the car."

"I'm seeing Deda," Gretel immediately responded, opening the door quickly and storming out of the truck, taking a more defiant tone than was indicative of how she actually felt. She had every intention of seeing her grandfather though. It had been months since she'd seen him, and even though she often felt awkward around him lately, more so now that he had worsened, she loved him enormously, and still considered him, next to her mother, the most comforting person in her world. If there was one person she needed right now, other than her mother, it was Deda.

She ran toward the house and as she reached the stoop she saw the tall, smiling figure of Deda standing in the doorway. She screamed at the sight of him. He looked so old, at least twenty years older than the seventy-five he actually was, and his smile was far from the thin-lipped consoling grin Gretel would have expected. Instead his mouth was wide and toothy, as if he had been laughing. He looked crazy, she thought.

"Hi, Deda," she said swallowing hard. "How are you feeling?"

At the sound of Gretel's voice, Deda's face lit up, morphing to normalcy and becoming consistent with that of a man seeing his beloved granddaughter for the first time in four months. "Gretel!" which he pronounced 'Gree-tel,' "my love, come in! Where is your brother?"

"He's in the car sleeping," she replied, and with that her brother came running into the house and into Deda's arms, which Deda had extended just in time to receive his grandson.

Deda held Hansel's shoulders and pushed him away to arms length. "Ahh, Hansel, you look so big!"

"You look really old, Deda," Hansel said, as respectfully as an eight-year-old could say such words.

Deda laughed, "I am so old, Hansel! I am so old!" He placed his palm on the back of the boy's neck and led him to the small sofa which was arranged just off the foyer. Deda sat down and lifted Hansel to his lap; Gretel followed and sat beside him on the cushion.

"Hello, Heinrich," Deda said, not taking his eyes from the children.

Gretel's father stood at the door, silently watching the interaction between his children and his wife's father. "Marcel."

"Why don't you sit?"

"We won't be staying."

Over the years Gretel had grown used to this style of conversation between her father and Deda, terse and factual, completely devoid of style. It wasn't that they disliked each other exactly, but more that they had failed to reach the level of trust normally achieved between two people at this stage in a relationship. Her parents had been married almost twenty years.

"Have you contacted The System?" Deda asked.

"Of course. They won't do anything for days," Gretel's father replied. And then, "Unless there's evidence of a crime."

Deda nodded in understanding. "Gretel," he said, "why don't you and your brother explore in the cellar for a while. I've some new books you would both like, just at the bottom of the stairs, on the first shelf there. You'll see them when you go down."

Deda stood and led the children to the cellar door, opening it and pulling the ribbed metal chain that hung just at the top of the stairs, unleashing a dull orange glow of light. The cellar was an obvious suggestion so that Deda could speak to her father alone, but Gretel didn't mind, and played along for her brother's sake. Besides, they were going to discuss her mother—and the possibilities of what might have happened—and she didn't have the emotional stamina to handle that right now.

As she and her brother reached the bottom of the cellar, Gretel saw that the books Deda referenced were the same ones he had had for at least two years now: Reptiles of the Northlands, Sea Life, and a few others containing topics Gretel had long since lost interest in.

"These books aren't new," Hansel complained. "I've read these a thousand times."

"Your Deda's old Han, he doesn't remember" Gretel replied, "And, anyway, you still like them."

"Fine."

Hansel opened the sea creature book absently and slumped heavily into a dusty club chair, once the centerpiece of Deda's living area but now in exile, having been replaced by a chair more conducive to Deda's frail condition. The dust from the chair puffed into the dim light and then dissipated. Normally Gretel found places like Deda's cellar repulsing—the dust was as thick as bread and seemed not to be spared from any section of furniture; and the scurrying sounds that clattered from the corners of the dark room conjured in her mind pictures of things much larger than mice. And she was sure that the spiders she had seen over the years had to be as large as any in the world.

But for all the impurities, Gretel had no memory of ever fearing the cellar. Lately, in fact, she felt drawn to it, mystified by the shrouded hodgepodge of books and tools and bric-a-brac that coated the surface of every shelf and table. There were candles and candle holders next to decorative plates and stemware; prehistoric preserve jars being used as paperweights for pictures of men and women Gretel had never seen in person; and dozens of other trinkets and curiosities that as a small girl she had considered junk—nuisances that cluttered up what might otherwise have been a play room for tea parties and dancing and such—but that she had recently come to admire.

The cellar, however, for all its antique charm, was also dark and difficult to explore. There was no window, and the one low-watt bulb that hung by the door illuminated only the area a few feet past the base of the steps; beyond that, a flashlight was required to make out any details of an object, if not just to walk. Gretel never asked Deda why he hadn't put a working lamp in the area, and now assumed it was to discourage her and Hansel from playing back there, though he had never explicitly forbade them from exploring that part of the house. Besides, as large as the cellar was, certainly large enough to convert into an apartment if Deda had ever decided to take in a boarder, most children didn't need to be warned about what may lurk in such a place.

But by eleven, and certainly now at fourteen, the illicitness of the "dark areas" only enhanced Gretel's curiosity, and, frankly, made the jaunts to Deda's bearable. What enjoyments she got at eight or nine were now almost completely nullified by her grandfather's health and her own adolescence. So the cellar had become her entertainment, and specifically the magazines.

Gretel found the flashlight that always sat on the seldom-used workbench and turned it on in Hansel's eyes.

"Stop, Gretel!"

Gretel chuckled. "I'm going to look for something in the back, I'll be right here, okay?" Gretel knew to be playful and delicate with her brother; he hadn't yet fully accepted that something bad might actually have happened to his mother, and if it occurred to him now, she thought, she was in no condition to help.

Hansel didn't respond, but looked up from the sea creatures book and followed Gretel with his eyes to the far end of the cellar, making sure the light was always visible.

Gretel felt her way to the antique bureau she was looking for and found the knob of the right-side drawer of the middle row. She could feel the weight of the magazines as she pulled, careful not to force the drawer and tear one of the covers. She pulled the top issue off the stack and thumbed through it, suddenly feeling nervous at the sight of the smiling, underclad women flipping past her. She leafed through to the end and put the first issue in the stack face down on the surface of the bureau so as to keep them in order when she put them all back, and took out the next issue, passively thumbing through it, staring at the women who were pretty much all the same. They weren't nude, but they were certainly there to provoke men and not to sell undergarments.

Gretel wasn't exactly sure why the women fascinated her. She didn't like girls in that way—at least she didn't think so—she certainly didn't get the same feelings looking at these women that she got when talking with certain boys at school. It was something else, something about their expressions. The way they smiled so easily for the camera when, Gretel had to assume, they felt ashamed and sad the whole time. She wanted to hug them, befriend them, let them know that she was fascinated by them, by their strength to do what she could never imagine. And that they were beautiful.

"Gretel, what are you doing?" Hansel called from the stairs.

Gretel flinched, nearly dropping the magazine, before fumbling it back to its proper place in the drawer and stacking the first one on top of it. "Nothing Han, looking at some old magazines. I'm coming."

She shut the bureau drawer and turned back for the stairs, and as the flashlight turned with her, the beam strayed wildly, just drifting over the thick black spine of a book. *The* book.

There it was.

The thick hardcover tome had presided from the top of Deda's tallest bookshelf for as long as Gretel had a memory of the house, which was from about age four. At that time, of course, the book was as mysterious and out of reach as space, and she hadn't the slightest clue as to what it might contain. But its sheer size and blackness had fascinated her even then.

The cover was absolute in its darkness, with no shine or reflection, as if it were overlaid with black wool. And there was no text or pattern on the spine—which was the only part Gretel would ever see for many years—and she imagined that someone looking up casually at the shelf could easily have mistaken the book for emptiness, a large gap in the middle of other books.

By age seven she got up the nerve to touch the book, which was no easy task given the height of the shelf and the book's position. It required delicate stacking of furniture and the tip-toe balance of a ballerina, but Gretel was determined, and soon became quite adept with her scaffolding.

During those years Gretel visited Deda's house regularly—at least once every other month—and with every visit she made a point to feel the book, to physically touch it, rubbing her fingertips on the exposed area. It was always cold—as were all of the books in the cellar—and its lack of any real texture, Gretel believed, gave an indication as to its age.

But she didn't touch the book because of any particular enchantment, or even because she thought it was magic, she did so more as a gauge, testing when she would be able to move forward on her stalled curiosity. As she grew taller, and as her level of comfort on the far ledges of stacked stools and empty milk crates increased, she began trying to flip the book out of its snug resting spot, placing her index finger at the top where the spine met the pages and then pulling backwards. At seven it never budged, as if cemented down, and the effort only enhanced Gretel's wonderment. It would be two years later when she would finally free the massive text and learn a word that would eventually come to hold a high place in her lexicon forever.

Gretel turned and faced the bookshelf and centered the beam of the flashlight on the book, which was no longer in its normal far left position on the top shelf, having moved to one center-right. In ten years it was the first time she had ever seen it out of place, other than when she was perusing it of course. Had it been in its current position when she was seven years old, she noted, it would have been a much easier endeavor to pull the book down, since this particular side of the shelf was far easier to access.

Now, at fourteen, the trick was to grab the book without attracting her brother's attention.

Gretel could see Hansel sifting through some boxes on the shelves near the stairs, and knew that his boredom would draw him to her soon; but the book was just out of her reach, and she didn't want to risk arousing his inquisitiveness by struggling and groaning on her tiptoes. Careful not to make any sudden motions, she pulled a large bucket from under the old wash basin and tossed aside a crusty towel that had dried crumpled and deformed inside, probably sometime in the last decade.

Gretel then placed the flashlight on the workbench, beacon down, reducing her visibility to a small halo of light on the table surface, and blindly flipped the bucket on its rim.

"Hey, what are you doing?" Hansel cried, his voice dripping with suspicion.

"Hansel, don't come over here, you'll trip on something," Gretel replied, trying to sound casual.

The sudden darkness had alerted her brother and Gretel silently cursed herself. She could hear him making tentative steps toward the bookshelf and Gretel quickly stepped up on the bucket, nearly missing the bottom brim and toppling to the floor. She began feeling for the black leather. She couldn't even make out the shadowy forms of the books without the flashlight, let alone any of the writing, but there was no doubt she would know her book by touch.

"Gretel?" Hansel again, edging closer.

"Han, I'm very serious, there are a million things that you could fall on and hurt yourself."

"I'll hold the light for you so you can see."

"I don't need the light, I've got it."

Gretel continued to feel for the book knowing she must be close. If it were in its proper spot she would have gotten it already and been done with it, now all this commotion would force her to make up some story about it. It didn't matter, he couldn't read the book anyway. She couldn't even read it. In fact, she couldn't even read the letters.

Gretel moved her hand over from a thin laminated book, and as instantly as the forefinger of her left hand brushed the cold, dead leather, she knew she had found it. By now Hansel had reached the shelf and was looking up at Gretel on the bucket.

"Han, shine the light up here," she barked in a loud whisper. "I don't want to knock anything off."

Hansel placed his hand on the flashlight, but before he could lift it to aid in his sister's search, a large beam of light shone in from the stairs, illuminating her face and the goal of her quest.

"Ah yes," her grandfather said, pointing the hanging bulb toward Gretel, "that book. It fascinates me, too."

CHAPTER THREE

THE FIRST BITE OF CHILL came down just before the top of the red sun slipped behind the tallest cedars. Darkness was less than an hour away, and the waking moon was already visible, waiting to take its post in the night sky.

Anika Morgan hunkered in a small, weathered-out cavity that had formed in a hill bank and covered her face with her hands. She was lost and had not the faintest concept of where the treeline might be. The hope that had carried her through clearings and creeks, over countless bluffs and damp wastelands, was gone.

At least for today.

Her will had shut down and the prospect of death was now lodged tightly in her brain. What had she done? To her children? Her husband? Her life? In her unruliest imagination she wouldn't have seen herself like this! Dying in the woods of the Northlands. She lamented once again her decision to plunge unprepared into these strange woods, knowing full well that map reading and orienteering were a glaring weakness in her skill set.

But her instincts to survive—if not to navigate—seemed to be properly aligned. She knew she hadn't the skills to trap or make fire, but early on Anika recognized the unlikelihood of escaping the forest in the daylight, and had wasted no time seeking shelter. Hunger had come calling hours ago, and she had kept an eye out for anything that could pass for food. But the elements, she knew, were her biggest threat, even in the midst of a mild spring day.

And she had been fortunate to find the 'cave,' which was how she thought of it, though it was really nothing more than a deep indentation in the side of a hill she'd been following for the last several hours. It was barely deep enough to sit in, let alone lie down, but it was shelter, and it would protect her from the cold night wind that was sure to come. The breezes she so welcomed during the heat of the day now terrified her.

A shiver scurried the length of Anika's back, the night again teasing what lie ahead, and Anika tucked her arms into the sleeves of her thin cotton blouse, gripping the bottoms of her elbows, her forearms layered across her abdomen below her bra. This was a bad sign, she thought: the sun had not fully set and the early stages of hypothermia had already begun. If she made it through the night, it wouldn't be without the help of God. Somewhere in the back of her mind she considered that her faith would help, but she would conserve her prayers for now, knowing the worst of the cold was still to come. What she wouldn't give for a blanket.

Anika drifted to sleep but was awake within minutes, the result of another short, epileptic shiver. She was wide-eyed and focused for a minute, and then drifted away again, repeating this cycle on and off for what may have been an hour, with her shakes each time becoming increasingly violent, as her muscles tried desperately to create warmth. She needed to move.

She crawled from the cave and stood outside in the open of the forest. It was dark, but not as dark as she would have imagined this far from civilization; the moon, thankfully, doing its part for her on this night.

She got to her feet and forced herself to run, at first in place, and then occasionally in short bursts to about a ten-foot radius, making sure not to lose sight of her shelter. She lifted her knees as high as possible, feeling the blood in them resist, and then start to come alive. The short naps had been frustrating and alarming—with death being the result of any deep sleep, she feared—but they had momentarily revived her, and Anika suddenly felt she could sustain the exercise long enough to get warm again. After that she wasn't sure, and she knew running around wasn't the long-term solution to her situation—after all, she was hungry, and her energy would fail soon. But for now running felt good, and she went with it.

The crunch of her shoes on the leaf litter and dry twigs sounded abrupt and panicky in the stillness of the forest, and the noise evoked in her some long-forgotten sense of urgency, the primal need to continue even under dire conditions and the harshest of circumstances. Though being lost in the woods in early spring, Anika conceded, hardly qualified as the 'harshest of circumstances.'

She felt suddenly energized, and desperately wished it were daytime so she could continue her lonely journey, ill-fated though it may be. She even considered, with the brightness of the moon, moving on at night; but her hunger, which was manageable now, wouldn't stay in the shadows for much longer, and if delirium was coming, she'd rather it arrive in the relative safety of her new burrow or in the light of day and not in the open of the forest darkness. Besides, if she did brave the forest tonight and was unable to find a cabin or some other artificial structure, it was unlikely she would again find natural accommodations like those she had now and would almost certainly freeze.

No, for now she would stay awake and keep her body moving as long as possible, conserving her water and resting when necessary. The night had a long way to go, but she felt she could make it.

Anika continued her pattern of light jogging, followed by short bursts of sprints, and then rest. As her legs began to tire, the jogging and sprint sessions became indistinguishable, and the rest periods became dozes. She resisted the urge to lie down, or huddle back in the cave, but sleep was inevitable.

THE LOUD CRUNCH OF feet startled Anika, and with semi-cognizance she chuckled to herself, realizing she had fallen asleep while somehow walking in place. Wouldn't that be a great ability to have right now, she thought, and then realized she was doing it now, which inspired her in a groggy, abstract sort of way. Maybe she could figure out how to harness this newfound talent and sustain it.

The dreamlike concept turned to alert curiosity, and Anika opened her eyes to find herself lying in darkness on the ground in her "resting" spot. She wasn't sleepwalking, she was just sleeping. Mud and branches stuck to the side of her nose and lips, and something insectile quickly crawled its way up from the hairline at the back of her head toward the top of her scalp.

She scrambled to her feet and looked around, frantically ruffling her hair, trying in consternation both to rid herself of the parasite now nestled in her hair and to identify the potentially larger threat on the perimeter. Anika's slumbered eyes adjusted slowly to the night, and the once-bright moon had temporarily withdrawn behind a stray cloud cluster, making even the black forms of the trees virtually invisible. She was blind, and something was stalking her.

Her first thought was to climb, to locate the closest tree—fallen or otherwise—and get as high as possible. She was no great athlete, but she trusted her abilities given the situation. Besides, running was out of the question, since virtually any animal that she could think of would catch her easily before she took more than a few strides.

But if she were to get some height, Anika thought, maybe she could buy some time. Jab at whatever was after her with a stick or something and frustrate it until it gave up. Anika thought of wolves. Wolves couldn't climb trees could they? She'd heard somewhere that bears could, but were there really bears in these parts?

These initial plans and imaginings ran their course in a matter of seconds, and were quickly replaced with calmer, more reasonable thoughts. Anika now thought it much more likely that whatever was prowling her space was something more common and less deadly than a wolf or bear. A deer or fox perhaps. Maybe a moose. She stood her ground, motionless, now listening with conscious ears for the sound of steps to repeat.

She waited for what seemed like several minutes and then: Crunch. Crunch. Crunch.

The patient steps moved to Anika's left—perhaps ten yards away, maybe less—and then stopped.

Her guess of a deer now seemed most likely; the steps were heavy and deliberate—not the scurrying movements of a squirrel or rabbit—but not threatening either, secretive and apprehensive.

Anika breathed out for the first time in what must have been a full minute, and the passing thoughts of small game now made her stomach moan in hunger. She felt only slightly relieved, however, knowing the 'deer' could just as easily be one of a dozen other, less docile things, ready to pounce at any moment.

Anika slowly stooped down, blindly feeling for the largest stick in her immediate confines, which turned out to be a stray branch, two-feet long at most and no thicker than a billiard cue. She grabbed it and stood back up without moving her feet.

"Hello," she said softly, mildly aware that she was attempting to talk to what she had convinced herself was a deer.

The night answered back with only the distant chirping of crickets and the light rustle of the trees' topmost leaves. The moon had returned to the black sky, and Anika's eyes adjusted. She could now see the silvery reflection of the branches and rocks that crowded the area. If something large was still there, she would certainly see it when it moved.

Keeping as still as possible, Anika shifted her eyes from right to left, turning her head just slightly upon reaching the limits of her periphery.

Crunch! Crunch! Crunch!

This time the sound was plodding and aggressive with no pretense of stealth. Terrified, Anika turned toward the sound, and saw only a glimpse of something curved and dull smash down on her forehead, catching her brow above her left eye and splitting it like a grape.

Did you enjoy this sample from Gretel? Grab your copy today[1]

1.   https://www.amazon.com/Gretel-Book-One-spine-chilling-thrilling-ebook/dp/B01605OOL4/

What inspired Christopher Coleman to write The Sighting?

LIKE A LOT OF PEOPLE, I've always been kind of captivated by things like Bigfoot and the Loch Ness Monster and other cryptozoological creatures.

But what was always more interesting to me were the people who claimed to have had close encounters with these creatures.

Of course, I've no doubt many of those people were just making up the stories—probably the vast majority of them—but certainly not all, right?

Some small percentage of those men and women truly believe they saw something beyond what's known to exist on Earth.

And, maybe, just maybe, they even did. So for those people, those who are convinced that they know to be true what the rest of the world thinks is legend, how must their lives have been altered from their experience? That question was the inspiration for The Sighting.

If you enjoyed The Sighting, please leave a review.[1] Your review is vitally important and will help readers decide whether or not to purchase The Sighting.

---

1.   https://www.amazon.com/Sighting-gripping-horror-psychological-thriller-ebook/dp/B076MJ5GVC/

CPSIA information can be obtained
at www.ICGtesting.com
Printed in the USA
FSHW011938291018
53406FS